POLLY PECORINO

WALKER
BOOKS

First published 2021 by Walker Books Ltd
87 Vauxhall Walk, London SE11 5HJ

This edition published 2023

2 4 6 8 10 9 7 5 3 1

LONDON BOROUGH OF RICHMOND UPON THAMES		identified as rted in accordance Act 1988
90710 000 546 619		ınd Mrs Ant
Askews & Holts	06-Apr-2023	ɔydon CR0 4YY
JF		ɔe reproduced, system in any
RTWH		ınical, including rior written

permission from the publisher.

British Library Cataloguing in Publication Data:
a catalogue record for this book is available from the British Library

ISBN 978-1-5295-0295-4

www.walker.co.uk

POLLY PECORINO

THE GIRL WHO RESCUES ANIMALS

Emma Chichester Clark

WALKER
BOOKS

 CHAPTER 1

Some people can pass a fly drowning in a puddle, or a beetle battling for its life on the surface of a swimming pool, and some can't. The ones that can't are rescuers. If you've ever stopped to save a fly or a beetle, or some other struggling creature, then you are probably a rescuer too.

Polly Pecorino was a constant rescuer. From the moment she took her first tottering steps she was knee-deep in puddles, saving lives. The first creature she ever saved was a daddy-long-legs. She fished it out of her mother's banana frappé.

You would never have guessed from looking at her that there was anything unusual about Polly. She looked like an ordinary schoolgirl, with brown hair and brown eyes. She liked doing all the usual things that schoolgirls do, and didn't like doing plenty of the other usual things too – particularly homework. But there *was* something unusual about Polly. As well as rescuing animals, she could actually talk to them – including birds and insects, and even amphibians, especially frogs. It was like being able to speak another language without having to learn it. (It made her feel better about not being very good at French.)

Polly couldn't explain how she did it and she didn't try to because most people wouldn't have believed her, and the rest might have thought she was showing off. That meant hardly anybody knew about her gift – only her parents and her Uncle Stan, even though she used it all the time. Sometimes she'd be in the middle of breakfast with her parents and she might hear the tiniest cry or the shrillest shriek of a creature in pain. Then she'd jump up without warning and rush out to the garden, returning later, having saved a life. It could have been a fledgling that had toppled out of its nest, or perhaps a tiny shrew trapped in a flowerpot. If the creature was injured, Polly did her best to nurse it back to health.

This was how Polly had first met Crow. One early morning, when she'd been in the middle of a dream about ring-tailed lemurs, she'd been woken by piercing cries. She'd thrown on her clothes and run straight out into the pouring rain. She'd found the crow half a mile away, in the park. He had fallen from an old chestnut tree and was

scrambling around in a muddy puddle, trying
to stand, falling, trying again, falling, all while
flapping his scrappy wings. He was panicking. He
couldn't get out of the puddle.

Polly looked for his parents or any sign of
his nest but couldn't see either. She reckoned he
was a long way from home, so she scooped him
up, wrapped him in her cardigan and took him
with her. He didn't struggle or make a fuss.

Back at her house, when she examined
him, she found he had a broken leg
and was suffering from shock. So
after making him a little splint,
which she taped to his leg with
Elastoplasts, she carried him
about with her for the rest
of the day, warm against
her chest.

He'd been so frightened by what had
happened to him that it wasn't until later that
evening he'd eventually spoken to her, and Polly

gathered that he'd been flying alone for the first time. He'd wanted to try out his wings and explore, to soar above the trees the way he'd seen the other crows do. His parents had told him to wait – because he wasn't ready – but he just couldn't wait any longer. And flying had been such a wonderful feeling, he told her, except he hadn't expected the wind to be so fierce.

"It was fighting me! It was twisting all my feathers!" he said. "And that's when I fell and landed in the puddle."

Polly kept the crow with her all through the following fortnight, taking him wherever she went, apart from school, when he stayed in her bedroom. It wasn't ideal, as Polly's mother

often said, because as his leg mended, the crow
became more energetic and daring and, especially,
inquisitive. Polly never knew what to expect when
she came home. More than once she'd found the
contents of her drawers and cupboards scattered
all over the floor.

At the end of the two weeks, Polly took Crow
to see her Uncle Stan, who was an expert on
animals. First, Stan checked his leg, which he said
was healing nicely, and then he gently stretched
out one of Crow's wings to have a look. "Well,"
he'd said. "They probably do need a bit more time
to grow before he flies." He smoothed out the
longest feathers. "They'll soon be strong enough.
He's lucky he has you to look after him."

Polly had known that when Crow's leg was better and his wings were bigger, she would have to let him go. He was a wild creature and he would need to live in the wild world he came from.

When the time came to release him, they went to the top of a nearby hill so that he could see all around and choose a direction to fly in. Polly prepared herself to say goodbye and Crow eventually swooped away, unsteadily, towards the trees.

Moments later, he swooped back and landed on her head.

"Aren't you going?" Polly had asked.

"I'd prefer to stay, if I may?" he replied.

And so he stayed.

CHAPTER 2

Polly and Crow lived in a small town called
Abbeville. It sat on the side of a wide valley,
overlooking a lake, known as Silent Water. All
the way round the valley there were woods,
stretching up into the mountains. On the furthest
side of the valley, across the lake, was Wild
Bear Woods. Nobody ever went there. There
were real wild bears living in the woods and
everyone in Abbeville was terrified of them.

They didn't even want to talk about them. Just the word "bear" was enough to send shivers down a townsperson's back. Long ago, they had built high walls around the town to protect themselves, and the gates were shut and locked each evening.

Even Polly, who loved animals, was very frightened of the bears in Wild Bear Woods. She often thought she could hear them – it was the only downside to her brilliant gift. At night, when everyone else was asleep and everything was quiet, Polly lay awake listening to the distant rumblings and roars. Sometimes she had nightmares of being chased through dark tangled woods. She'd be running and running, feeling the bears close behind her, their long yellow claws catching on her clothes, and her legs would suddenly crumple, and she'd stumble and fall. Then she'd wake up, in her own safe warm bed, with her heart pounding in her chest.

She knew there were terrible stories about the bears, about their ruthlessness and ferocity and the dreadful things that happened to the people who met them, but no one would tell her anything specific.

Polly thought that sometimes not knowing something was far worse than knowing the truth, however terrible, so one day, after a particularly bad nightmare, she asked Uncle Stan about the bears. "I need you to tell me everything you know," she said. "You have to tell me!"

Crow hopped from foot to foot on her shoulder, as agitated as she was.

Stan looked at Polly uncertainly. "Well, I suppose you're old enough now." He took off his hat and held it to his chest. "There are lots of stories about the bears, but I suppose the worst … the scariest … is about the family who stopped in Wild Bear Woods for a picnic." He stopped talking and gripped his hat even more tightly.

"Go on!" said Polly.

"Apparently, it gets very dark in there very quickly," Stan continued. "The edges of the wood don't look so bad, but inside, the trees grow so densely, and the branches are thick and all woven together, so that the sun can't get in and you can't see much. It's dark as night all day long, they say, and this family must have got lost, and … they wouldn't have seen the hole … and they fell … they fell into a pit … deep, really deep, like a well…"

Stan continued in a whisper, "But it wasn't a well. It was a trap. It was the bears' trap—" he gulped— "to catch humans."

Polly gasped. "How horrible!"

"The family," Stan said, "Mum, Dad, Grandma and four children – they all fell in together, and they were all eaten, one by one, over a week."

"That's so gruesome!" whispered Polly.

"Gruesome is right. And worst of all, it's not the first time it's happened. Others have gone missing too—" he gulped again— "but I mustn't scare you any more … and that's why you must never, ever, ever go outside the town walls at night."

CHAPTER 3

Set on the highest point of Abbeville, inside the town wall, on the opposite side to Wild Bear Woods, was Happy Days Zoo. It had once been the pride of the county. People had come from far and wide to see the collection of rare and beautiful animals that had been bred there. Unlike the bears of Wild Bear Woods, these animals were never frightening (except when they pretended to be) because they loved the company of humans. But when the owner died, the zoo had been passed on to a couple called Dolores and Albert Snell, who sadly did not care for the animals in the same way.

So, nowadays, Happy Days Zoo had an air of neglect. Nothing was ever repaired or replaced. Weeds rambled over paths, and the Snells, keen to save money, had "let go" of many of the old zookeepers who had loved and tended the animals for years. Even the animals had lost their sheen. Their eyes were dull, their coats, duller. They were old and tired.

Nobody wanted to hear the wail of a woebegone wolf, or see the penguins waddling aimlessly round their dirty concrete pool, so they stayed away.

Stan had worked at the zoo for many, many years. He had hand-reared most of the animals and he'd seen the zoo through plenty of changes, but none as bad as this.

The sight of the zoo made Polly very sad, and she longed to help the animals. As soon as she was old enough, Stan took Polly to the zoo with him. Polly's parents, Mr and Mrs Pecorino, owned a restaurant in the next town, a few miles away, and they were always busy – buying food, growing food, cooking food and racing all over the county in their little van with the Il Pecorino logo on the side to find special ingredients. They worked so hard it was difficult for them to keep an eye on Polly. If it hadn't been for Stan and Crow, Polly would have been alone most of the time. She helped Stan at the zoo nearly every day after school, and all the time through the school holidays.

"How would I manage without you?" Stan would say, when he brought her animals that were sick, or just seemed unhappy, so she could ask them what was wrong. There was so much to do at the zoo, and there was nearly always some sort of problem waiting for Polly when she arrived – a sickly seal, a gloomy gibbon, a tapir that wouldn't eat because its food was mouldy. Sometimes Polly found it almost heartbreaking.

She tried as hard as she could to make a difference, but there was only so much she could manage. Most of all, she just listened. Nearly all of the animals needed to talk.

"If only you knew..." The aardvark's gentle eyes clouded with tears.

"I just don't think I can stand it any more!" cried a lemur, clutching Polly's hand in its small silvery fingers.

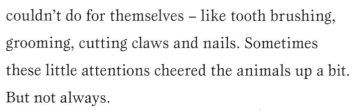

"It's so, so miserable here!" wailed an ostrich.

Polly tried to help with the small, practical things the animals couldn't do for themselves – like tooth brushing, grooming, cutting claws and nails. Sometimes these little attentions cheered the animals up a bit. But not always.

"Let's brush your hair!" she'd suggest to an orangutan.

"What's the point?" he'd answer sadly. "Who cares?"

"I care," Polly would answer. "And it will make you feel better."

And, usually, after she'd done it, the orangutan did feel better, for a while.

Here and there, Polly gave the animals medicines or tonics or vitamin supplements, but there was never enough of anything. When things ran out, she sometimes used her own pocket money to buy more. She and Stan did whatever they could think of to improve things, but whatever they did, it never seemed to be enough. They often felt quite overwhelmed and useless because they couldn't change anything. It was out of their control.

"Do you think the Snells really don't care about the animals?" Polly asked Stan one day.

"I'm afraid they don't," said Stan sadly.

"But Mr Snell cares about his cat." Polly wrinkled her nose as she pictured the cat lying on his velvet cushion. The creature had long, matted brownish-coloured fur and a squashed-up face that always looked disagreeable. He was a bad-tempered and unlovable creature, in Polly's opinion. She'd never had a conversation with him and was grateful that he'd clearly decided to ignore her from day one. His name was Poodywoo.

"He's besotted with him," agreed Stan.

"So how can he not care about the others? I don't think he means to be unkind to them, do you?" asked Polly.

"No, perhaps not. But his wife is the boss and…" Stan shivered and tailed off as if he couldn't bear to finish that sentence.

"I don't think Mrs Snell is a kind person, is she?"

Stan shivered again. "No … I'm afraid you're right. She's not a very nice person at all."

 # CHAPTER 4

Albert Snell had never, ever, in a million years, expected to inherit a zoo. He had never even met the great-aunt who left it to him and he had never heard of Abbeville either.

Before he'd taken over Happy Days Zoo, Mr Snell had a boring job in a boring accountancy firm in the city. The only remarkable thing about him was the number of stains he managed to collect on his nasty suit and tie. His clothes were splattered with almost every meal he had ever eaten.

His messy eating habits were, in fact, how he had met his wife, Dolores. It was at the Annual Accountancy Ball and she was waitressing. When Mr Snell dribbled consommé down his evening shirt, Dolores mopped him up and tied a napkin around his neck. Poor Mr Snell, unused to attention of any kind, had been enraptured and told her all about the zoo he'd inherited, to make himself seem important. Dolores immediately thought that owning a zoo must mean he was very rich, so she had sat down in the empty chair beside him.

"Tell me more," she purred, and for a moment she reminded Albert Snell of his beloved cat, Poodywoo, the only creature in the world that he loved.

He had told her all about his doubts and fears over running the zoo.

"You'll be marvellous," she said. "You're just the man for it. I can't imagine anyone better!"

"But I'm not that fond of animals, apart from my cat," he admitted.

"Ah, you have a dear little cat? Then of course you like animals. You love animals, and I'm sure they love you!"

Albert Snell had gazed at the vision that was Dolores – this beautiful woman who understood him so well – and he knew she must be right. He could run the zoo – but only with her at his side. She was an angel, sent to save him, and he fell head over heels in love. Or, at least, he thought he did.

As for Dolores, she decided right there and then that Albert Snell was her Golden Ticket. She didn't want to be a waitress any more. She wanted cocktails and sunsets on golden beaches in faraway places. She longed for a giant TV screen

and leopard-print leisurewear, and a huge pool
that she could swim in every day. Her favourite
thing was aqua aerobics – she'd be able to splash
about as much as she liked and never have to
work again!

In fact, that night, they both imagined that
they had been rescued and that from then on it
was going to be Happy Ever After and singing and
dancing in the moonlight. But they were wrong.
They were completely and absolutely wrong, of
course, because nothing is ever quite that simple,
is it?

 CHAPTER 5

Even though Mr Snell had been an accountant, he wasn't any good at sums. You really should be good at counting money, adding it up and making it grow, if you are running a zoo – or any kind of business. So, very soon after they'd got married, Dolores realized he was hopeless. She told him this at least twenty-five times a day.

"You are absolutely HOPELESS, Albert!" she said.

"I had no idea you were so USELESS, Albert!" she sighed.

"You are an absolute DUNDERHEAD, Albert!" she snarled.

Her words echoed in his ears all day long.

Mr Snell was becoming more and more frightened of Dolores because she was furious nearly all the time.

"Oh, Poodywoo!" Mr Snell sighed one afternoon. "Let's run away together!"

The cat sneered.

Mr Snell was sitting in his office at the zoo watching Poodywoo, who had just finished licking out a whole pot of double cream. Nobody understood why Mr Snell loved the cat so much because the cat didn't care about anybody in the world. But he was the light of Mr Snell's miserable life.

Mr Snell shuddered as he remembered how Dolores had stared at Poodywoo that morning. Normally, she didn't give the cat a second glance, but, earlier, she had been staring at him intensely, even longingly. She'd spoken quietly, as if thinking aloud, "Fabulous! Just fabulous. A perfect winter hat. Just my colour. Just my size…"

Mr Snell's blood had run cold. "Sorry, dear? What did you say?"

Mrs Snell had smiled. "Well, if there's no money to buy a new hat, I shall just have to make one." And her smile had widened as she'd looked at Poodywoo.

The cat flinched. Mrs Snell's startlingly white teeth almost blinded him.

"In fact," Mrs Snell added, "I've been thinking about how we might make all of the animals in the zoo easier to manage." She'd produced a business card from the pocket of her dress and put it on Mr Snell's desk.

> ### Guaranteed to bring you Lifelike Results!
>
> ARTHUR G. STRINGFELLOW
>
> **TAXIDERMIST**
>
> CALL TODAY! TEL: 0126789 2436478

Mr Snell had quickly looked up "taxidermist" in the dictionary when his wife wasn't watching. Under "taxidermy" it said: the art of preparing, stuffing and mounting the skins of dead animals so that they have a lifelike appearance.

"How can you even think such a thing?" he'd gasped.

Dolores had shrugged. "What's the point of continually feeding all these fleabags? If they were stuffed, all we'd have to do is dust them now and then."

Mr Snell shivered, recalling the earlier conversation. And what was she up to now? She'd seemed unusually cheerful – he'd even heard her singing. She'd said she was going to meet someone. "Who would that be, dear?" he'd asked timidly before she'd snapped his head off.

Mr Snell sighed. All he'd ever hoped for was a quiet life, to live "happily ever after" with his lovely wife and his darling Poodywoo. Why couldn't his life be like that? he wondered.

Was Dolores right about the taxidermy? Mr Snell pondered. Maybe she was. Most of the zoo's inhabitants looked worn out and moth-eaten. For some of them, it was all they could do to get up in the morning and hobble outside to see what the weather was like. Maybe he'd be doing them a favour. And the visitors would surely prefer to see animals with glossy coats and shining glass eyes...

Mr Snell read the card again and picked up the phone.

 CHAPTER 6

The door burst open and Dolores appeared.
Poodywoo's tail thrashed violently from side to side.

"I'm about to call them, dear!" Mr Snell
waved the card at her.

"Forget about that!" snapped Mrs Snell.
"You'll be glad to hear that my meeting has
produced the most marvellous results!"

Mr Snell hardly recognized his wife. Her face
was glowing with excitement. She ushered in two

boys wearing hoodies. They were carrying a sack. Poodywoo patrolled along the edge of the desk. He hissed at Mrs Snell.

"Oh, go away!" Mrs Snell swatted the cat with a rolled-up newspaper.

The boys dumped the sack on the floor. Poodywoo slunk away, giving Mrs Snell one last venomous look, but she didn't notice.

"What is that?" asked Mr Snell.

Everyone ignored him.

"We'll take fifty quid for it!" said the larger of the two boys.

"Twenty!" snapped Dolores.

"Thirty-five!" said the boy.

"Done!" said Dolores. She grabbed the boy's hand and shook it before he could change his mind.

A mournful sound was coming from the sack, which began to rock backwards and forwards.

"Can you get any more?" asked Dolores.

"You got to be jokin'!" said the larger boy. "I ain't going back there!"

"I'd make it worth your while." Dolores smiled her sparkliest of smiles.

"Just give us the money!" said the shorter boy.

"Now!" hissed the other one, thumping his fist on the desk in front of Mr Snell, who jumped but said nothing.

The larger boy jerked a thumb in his direction. "What's the matter with 'im?" he asked. "Oi! You! What you doin'? Catchin' flies?"

Mr Snell closed his mouth quickly.

"If only he were that useful!" said Mrs Snell wearily. She shoved a handful of notes at the boy. "Here's your money. Now get lost! Au revoir! And don't let me see you round here again!"

The boy pushed the notes into his back pocket and pulled his hood further over his face. "Nice doin' business with you!" He and the other boy lurched towards the door.

When they'd gone, Mrs Snell prodded the sack with her pointy toe. "This is the answer to all our prayers, Albert." She began to giggle. The giggle turned into snorts.

Albert had never heard her make those sounds before. "I don't see why you can't just tell me what it is," he said crossly.

Mrs Snell hummed to herself as she applied a layer of crimson to her lips. "I have some phone calls to make." She pointed to the sack. "I want you to keep an eye on that until I'm back."

"On what, dear?" said Albert.

Mrs Snell rolled her eyes. "Don't let it out of your sight!" she snapped.

Mr Snell clicked his heels together and saluted. "Certainly, dear!" he said sarcastically.

When she'd gone, Mr Snell edged around to the front of the desk and stared at the sack. It was tied with blue twine. It was still rocking.

He kneeled down and pulled on one end of the twine. The sack fell open. Mr Snell couldn't see inside, so he stood up and took a large step backwards – just in case it was something dangerous – and then he lifted the edge of the sack with his toe.

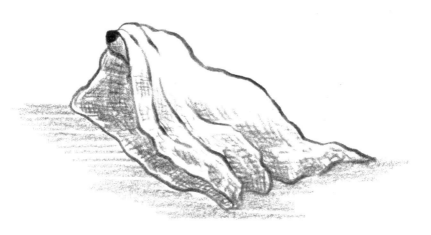

A shiny black nose pushed its way out.
It sniffed the air, up and down and side to side,
and came to a stop in front of Mr Snell. Mr Snell
held his breath. The edge of the sack slid back
a little further to reveal a small brown snout.
Then it slid back a little more, and two bright
unblinking eyes glared up at him.

Now he could see the whole face, the eyes, the
ears and the teeth...

He stumbled backwards and sat down heavily
on the edge of the desk. For a moment, everything
stopped. Then he blinked and rubbed his eyes and
looked down at the sack again. The thing inside
hadn't moved.

"Oh, my! Oh, my!" Mr Snell whispered. He felt as if he couldn't breathe. His heart was pounding. He was afraid he might have a heart attack. He tried to take deep breaths in and out, slowly.

The creature still hadn't moved, and Mr Snell began to wonder if it was all right. After all, it was only a tiny thing – just a baby, really – and there was something rather fascinating about it...

What had Dolores said? The answer to our prayers...

"Oh, my!" he gasped. "She's right!"

And a hundred thoughts came rushing at him – visions of cash! Visions of ticket sales! Dring! Dring! He could hear the tills ringing. No one had ever captured one before. There'd be queues round the block, publicity, newspapers, television – they'd be rich! They'd be famous! Dolores would stop being cross! Poodywoo would have caviar! They'd all have caviar!

The possibilities seemed endless. He'd always wanted to go on a cruise... Perhaps now, they could – the Caribbean – he could see Dolores standing on the deck, one hand on the rail… He could see her slipping… Oh! Oh! Going over…

Mr Snell began to laugh. He laughed and laughed. It felt so good. Tears poured down his cheeks and in a wild gesture of joy he swept all the papers off his desk. He wanted to hug Dolores, but she wasn't there so, without thinking, he swooped down to hug the little creature in the sack – the source of all his new-found happiness! But it had seen him coming and it scrambled out, lickety-split, and bared its teeth. Then it leaped onto Mr Snell's shoulder and bit him, hard, on the ear.

"OW!" screamed Mr Snell.

CHAPTER 7

On the other side of the zoo, Polly and Crow were trying to patch up an old termite mound in the giant anteater's yard. "You're not helping, Crow!" cried Polly.

Crow had discovered that termites were unexpectedly delicious and kept eating them. This was making the old anteater increasingly irritated, and as the two of them fought over the grubs, the mound was crumbling faster than Polly could fill it.

"Crow! Stop!" cried Polly.

They were making so much noise, it was a miracle that Polly could hear anything at all, but suddenly she did hear something. It was the sound of a small voice she didn't recognize.

"Ssh! Crow! Stop!" said Polly again.

There it was once more: a small voice … in distress.

There were no words – just cries. Polly leaped to her feet and ran in the direction of the sound.

She followed it all the way through the Bamboo Village, past the Watering Hole, along the Caribbean Cove and round the Alabama Wilds until she was outside Mr Snell's office. That was where the sound was coming from.

Normally, she would have knocked, but this time Polly ran straight in.

It looked as though a tornado had blown through the room. There was a sea of paper all over the floor and Mr Snell was lying in the middle of it, his face ashen, his eyes darting from side to side. There was blood dripping from his ear.

"Catch it, Polly!" he gasped.

Polly was aware of a sudden movement. Something small and brown flashed past her from behind the desk. It disappeared behind the filing cabinet with a whimper, like a child crying.

"It's all right," she whispered. "Don't be afraid. I won't hurt you."

She kneeled down and peered behind the filing cabinet. Then she gasped. Two dark brown eyes stared back at her. Surely, it couldn't be... No. It couldn't be... No... It couldn't be a bear!

She felt cold all over. And frightened. How could there be a bear ... here ... in this room ... right here?

Polly glanced at Mr Snell, but he was quietly backing out of the office and pulling the door shut behind him.

The little creature cried out again. Polly wondered what to do. It was such a sad sound. It was a baby – a cub. It was lost. It needed her. But ... it was a bear!

The animal whimpered again and Polly made a decision.

"Come here." She stretched out her arms. "I won't hurt you." And I hope you won't hurt me, she added silently.

Little by little, the cub inched forwards until his face emerged from the shadows. He wiped a large paw across his nose.

Polly patted her knee. "Come here. Come on. It's quite safe."

The bear shuffled slowly towards Polly, over all the crumpled paper, and looked up into her eyes. Then he climbed onto her knee and pushed his wet, black nose into her neck and breathed deeply.

"There, there," whispered Polly.

She put her arms round him gently and rocked him. Her heart was beating very fast. She couldn't believe she was actually holding a bear – a real live bear! It might be only a baby, but it had very long claws, very long *sharp* claws! And it had extremely sharp teeth! How terrifying and dreadful a fully-grown bear would be.

"I don't know what you're doing here," Polly said softly, "or how you got here, but there's going to be trouble – big trouble, that's for sure."

She sat for a long time with the cub on her knee, rocking him and stroking his fur. She took long deep breaths to steady her nerves and gradually began to feel calmer. The bear relaxed too.

"Don't worry, little one," she said. "Don't be frightened. I'll take good care of you, I promise. Everything will be all right."

She went on talking to him quietly, although she guessed he was too young to have learned many words. Finally, she felt him grow heavy in her arms and saw that he'd fallen asleep. Then she

laid him on a cushion and put him in the bottom drawer of the filing cabinet. He looked peaceful.

Polly couldn't stop staring at him. She never thought she'd ever be able to look so closely at a real bear.

After a while, Polly tiptoed over to the phone on Mr Snell's desk and dialled Stan's extension. Seconds later, Stan knocked on the door, and when Polly opened it, she put her finger to her lips and pointed at the filing cabinet.

"Oh, no!" Stan went deathly white. "I don't believe it! How on earth…? The Snells…" He took off his cap and ran his fingers through his hair. "They must be out of their minds!"

CHAPTER 8

Polly and Stan found the Snells down near the main gate. Mr Snell was sitting on a bench eating an ice cream and trying to forget his sore ear. His wife was pacing back and forth, talking on her phone, her hand slicing the air one minute, punching it the next.

Stan marched towards Mr Snell. "Can you explain what's going on, Mr Snell? I'm sure it's only a temporary arrangement, isn't it? I mean, I'm sure you don't mean to keep a wild bear cub in your office, do you?"

Mr Snell did not reply. He was concentrating on his ice cream. There were already several drips on his trousers.

"Mr Snell!" said Stan. "This is very important! You do realize, don't you, that you can't possibly keep a wild bear here at the zoo?!"

"Of course we can!" Mrs Snell ended her phone call. "Cute, isn't he?"

"No, Mrs Snell! Not cute! Or, yes, maybe cute now, but this situation is very dangerous! This is a mistake! A catastrophic mistake!" Stan had gone very red in the face. Polly could see he was extremely upset.

"I'll help you sort it out," Stan went on, his voice shaking. "We'll get the bear back to where it belongs, as quick as possible, and everything will be all right!"

"DON'T BE RIDICULOUS!" snapped Mrs Snell.

Polly and Stan jumped.

"THAT CUB'S NOT GOING ANYWHERE!"

Mrs Snell glared at Stan and Polly. "Have you got spaghetti for brains? I am SAVING the zoo – single-handedly, it seems! WHAT IS WRONG WITH YOU?"

Polly and Stan backed away. They'd reached the fence when Mrs Snell bore down on them. Her face was so close, her red lips were almost touching Stan's nose.

"I see I'll have to spell it out for you."
Mrs Snell drew a long breath of air through
her polished teeth. "People don't want dreary,
depressed lions and moth-eaten llamas. They don't
want moping monkeys and pathetic penguins.
They don't want TAME animals. It's BORING!
They want something real, something wild,
something dangerous, something terrifying!"

She couldn't help smiling, her awful lips
stretched unnaturally. It was a moment before
she spoke again. "This exhibit will be the most
valuable and lucrative asset this miserable zoo
has ever had!"

"But, Mrs Snell…" said Stan. "That cub must
be returned! You're putting us all in danger!"

"Oh, don't be
ridiculous. It's a baby bear
and it will be kept under
the highest security at all
times. Twenty-four seven,"
snapped Mrs Snell.

"But don't you realize what you're doing? You're endangering the whole town!" cried Stan. "They'll come for him! THE BEARS WILL COME HERE! You can't do this, Mrs Snell!"

Mrs Snell wasn't listening. Neither was Mr Snell. He had put his fingers in his ears and was half-running, half-skipping towards the ticket office. They could hear his tuneless singing: "We paid for the bear and the bear will pay for us. Billions! Squillions! The bear will pay for us…"

Mrs Snell was on the phone again.

Polly looked at Stan. "What are we going to do? Will people really come to see a bear? I thought everyone was terrified of them?"

"Of bears in the wild, yes, but…" Stan sat down. He put his head in his hands. "The trouble is, people are fascinated by them too, and they'll jump at the chance to see a baby bear in a zoo if they think it's safe. But it's not! It won't be long until his wild bear family come for him!"

"So, what are we going to do, Uncle Stan?"

"I don't know, Polly. I really don't know."

CHAPTER 9

The bear's arrival was not a happy day for Polly or Stan at Happy Days Zoo. And there was worse to come.

Within a few days, the Snells had already made a lot of important decisions about the cub and its surroundings. They'd decided to splash out, for the first time in their lives, and spend some money on the old lion's den, which had sat empty for years. They were going to turn it into a state-of-the-art enclosure with open viewing areas surrounded by bars, deep water and high walls.

"We've got ourselves a little gold mine!" said Mrs Snell happily to her husband.

Mr Snell thought his wife almost looked as pretty as when they'd first met. "Well done, my little lovebird," he whispered and stretched a hand towards her, but she deftly avoided it with a flick of her wrist.

"That's enough, Albert!" she snapped.

Mr and Mrs Snell were not the most patient of people, as you might have guessed. They didn't give the builders a minute's peace while the new walls were being built.

"Time is money!" screamed Mrs Snell.

In fact, everything was done in just a few days, including employing the guards who were paid to watch over the cub's temporary cage.

Everyone had ignored the poor little creature in the rush to prepare his new prison – everyone, that is, apart from Polly, who couldn't forget about him, even though she wasn't allowed to visit him. He was in her thoughts day and night and she couldn't stop thinking about how homesick and unhappy he must be. She could only hope that he'd be happier when he had more space, but she knew it was unlikely.

The moving day soon came. Everything was ready. The revamped lion's den was now called "The Bear Garden". Mr Snell had thought of the name and was very pleased with himself. Outside the zoo, a sign said:

Come and see
our very own
WILD BEAR CUB!
See him play... See him dance...
You won't be disappointed!
HE'S ADORRRRRABEARAL!

The Snells watched from the viewing area
as four security guards wearing helmets wheeled
the cub's small cage into the middle of the Bear
Garden and put it beside a newly planted plastic
tree. Even Poodywoo was interested. He sauntered
along the top of the enclosure wall, flicking his
tail, but soon grew bored and went off to the
small mammal house where he enjoyed spooking
the hamsters.

Polly and Stan stood at a distance by the gate,
so that the Snells wouldn't notice them. They were
both very nervous. Stan had tried again and again
to talk to Mrs Snell about returning the bear to
the woods, but it had been no use.

After a few minutes, four more guards arrived, carrying shields and batons. Gingerly, they opened the door of the cage. Everyone held their breath and waited for the star to emerge ... but it didn't.

"Come on!" hissed Mrs Snell through clenched teeth.

There was no movement.

"GET HIM OUT!" Mrs Snell shook both her fists over her head. "USE YOUR BATONS, YOU DOZY NINCOMPOOPS!"

The four armed guards stood either side of the cage uncertainly. None of them moved. The other guards who had pushed the cage into the enclosure were standing far back.

"On the count of three," shouted Mrs Snell, "beat the bars! ONE ... TWO ... THREE!"

Polly watched with alarm as the guards raised their batons. But they lowered them very slowly, so that there was barely a sound when they touched the bars. Seemingly, none of them wanted to upset the cub.

"Unbelievable!" Mrs Snell said in a quiet, steady voice. Then she shouted, "ABSOLUTE FOOLS!" so loudly and so suddenly that one of the guards fell over. She glared at them all.

Finally, she marched down the steps of the viewing platform on her tippy-tappy heels, and round to the entrance of the Bear Garden. She grabbed two of the guards' batons, one in each hand, and she began to attack the bars of the cage with all her might.

"OUT! OUT! OUT!" she yelled.

The noise was terrible and terrifying, and the little bear hurtled through the open door at top speed. He crashed into the scrubby bushes and disappeared.

"Oh, no you don't!" cried Mrs Snell. "I haven't spent all this money for you to hide!" She looked as if she was about to dive into the bushes herself.

"Calm down," Mr Snell shouted from the viewing platform. "We've got him where we want him now. Let's leave him to get used to his new surroundings and come back later."

Mrs Snell made a sound like an angry bull and shook her fist at the bushes. Then she stomped out of the Bear Garden. Polly and Stan flattened themselves against the wall as they saw her coming.

When they'd gone, Stan went back to his work with the other animals, but Polly went up to the viewing platform and leaned over the wall. She looked for the cub in the enclosure below, but she couldn't see him anywhere. Crow flew down and skimmed the tops of the bushes.

She watched him
land clumsily on the
far side of the pool and
disappear into a clump
of reeds. A few minutes
later, he emerged and
flew back.

"Did you find him? Is
he all right?" asked Polly.

"Scared," said Crow. "Little scared baby."

Polly wanted to say something to help the
cub, but she didn't know what she could tell him
that would be truthful. How could she reassure
him when she felt so anxious herself? In the end
she shouted as loudly as she dared, "We'll do
everything we can for you, little bear. Crow and
I – we won't forget about you. And Crow will stay
with you tonight. We are listening out for you and
thinking about you all the time."

It didn't feel like much, but it was all she
could do.

As she walked home that evening, Polly felt uneasy. She had a headache and there was a buzzing sound in her ears. It had been there all day. At first, it had just felt a bit annoying. She'd shaken her head to clear her ears, but it had made no difference. Now, as she made her way down the street, it was growing louder.

Then Polly realized – it wasn't just a buzzing in her ears – it was roaring. It was the bears in Wild Bear Woods, roaring!

She'd heard the bears before, in the dead of night, but this was different. They were roaring with rage and fury, and they were so loud. They must be getting nearer, she thought. They must be moving through Wild Bear Woods towards Abbeville. Stan was right; they were going to come and get their cub. It could only be a matter of time and Polly suddenly felt very frightened.

CHAPTER 10

Next morning at Happy Days Zoo, Mrs Snell, followed by Mr Snell, marched to the Bear Garden and peered down from the viewing platform.

"WHERE IS IT?" Mrs Snell bellowed at the guards. "It had better not have escaped!"

"There's no way it could have," one guard answered. "It must still be hiding in the bushes."

Mrs Snell was furious. "We've spent all this money on the little blighter! I'm not having it wasted!"

"I'm sure it will all be…" Mr Snell began. He tailed off as Mrs Snell frowned at him. Then she spotted Stan on his way to the monkey house, carrying a box of bananas.

"WHAT ARE YOU GOING TO DO ABOUT THIS?" she yelled. "This bear is meant to be the most exciting exhibit the zoo has ever had and it's invisible! What are you going to do?"

"Me?" said Stan. "It's nothing to do with me!" And then a thought occurred to him. If he and Polly could just get close to the cub, maybe they could do something… They could get him out before the bears arrived at the zoo. "But if it were up to me," he added, "I'd get Polly."

"Polly?" asked Mrs Snell.

"You know, Dolores," said Mr Snell. "That girl who's always hanging around, with the crow."

"You think she can sort it?" asked Mrs Snell.

"If anyone can, she can," said Stan.

"Right!" said Mrs Snell. "Get Polly!"

Polly didn't need to be persuaded to come and help. She hadn't been able to stop thinking about the cub all night.

Crow had stayed with the cub since the day before and was still there when Polly arrived. She called to him as one of the guards unlocked the door to the enclosure. He had been practising his flying and it was definitely improving, apart from the landings, and he flew towards Polly as she came inside. The cub watched them from the bushes, where he was invisible to Mrs Snell.

"You make that wretched bear cub come out!" she shouted from the viewing platform, peering through an enormous pair of binoculars.

Polly didn't answer.

The cub continued to watch Crow, and Polly could see that they had struck up a friendship.

"Caw! Caw! Caw!" cried the crow.

"Caw! Caw! Caw!" squeaked the cub.

But when Polly took a step closer, the cub snarled and bared his teeth. Then he ran away, through the scrubby undergrowth, and disappeared from view. Polly hesitated, not sure what to do, but, forcing herself to be brave, she went after him. She found him in the concrete hut that had once been the lioness's bedroom.

The cub pressed himself against the wall in the darkest corner. Polly knew she was going to have to repair his trust in her; after all, she was a human being, and so far, all the humans he had met had treated him badly. She sat down against the opposite wall.

"I'm sorry you've had such an awful time," she said quietly. "I know it's been very frightening. I want to be your friend and help you."

The bear wouldn't look at her. She'd promised to look after him on that first day, in Mr Snell's office, but she hadn't been able to. Would he be able to trust her again?

Feeling sad and dejected, Polly gave up and went out to sit by the pool. Crow landed on her shoulder. "Any good?" he asked.

"Not really," said Polly. "But I'll keep trying."

In the evening, when it was time to go, Polly told the little cub she'd be back in the morning, leaving him with Crow again.

She had hoped to avoid Mrs Snell, but as she was walking to the main gate, Mrs Snell yelled at her and Polly froze. She came over to Polly and stood so close that Polly had to take a few steps back.

"You'd better have done what I told you!" she hissed. "You'd better have got that bear out!"

"Um … well, nearly…" whispered Polly.

"Nearly?" shouted Mrs Snell. "I didn't ask for nearly! If that bear is not out on display tomorrow, don't bother to come back! Do you hear me? Tomorrow! Or don't come back here ever again!"

When Polly arrived for her second day with the cub, he was still hiding in the undergrowth. Polly knew this was her last chance, and after the way the cub had reacted to her the day before, she was worried. He looked up, though, as she came into the Bear Garden, and instead of snarling and running away, he followed her, at a distance, to the pool. Polly sat under the shade of a large tree, so that she couldn't be seen from the viewing platform. The bear sat too. Then, gradually, he moved closer, inch by inch. When he was sitting right beside her, he rested his head against her. Polly hardly dared move. She felt overwhelmed with tenderness and sympathy for the little creature. She put her arm around him. After a while the bear told her his name was Booboo, and that he wanted to go home. He hadn't learned many words yet, as Polly had guessed, but he was able to tell her how sad he felt.

"Oh, Booboo," said Polly. "Whatever happens, I will be your friend – and Crow too. If I could take you home, I would. I really would, but I'm not allowed to. There are too many guards. They would stop us. I promise if there is ever a chance – I will."

The cub looked at Polly with his big frightened eyes. It was such an awful thing to have happened to so small a creature. If only she could get him past those guards. But it was impossible.

And in any case, how could she take Booboo back to Wild Bear Woods? How would she ever find his parents before being eaten by his cousins and aunts first?

But Polly knew that if she didn't act, the bears would come to Abbeville. The roaring sounds from Wild Bear Woods were getting louder and closer. It wouldn't be that hard for the bears to find a way in. They could climb trees, so they could probably climb walls, couldn't they?

She knew, for sure, that the town was in terrible danger. People's lives were at risk!

Polly shivered. She had to do something – but what?

 **CHAPTER 11**

As soon as the Snells saw that the little cub had ventured out of the bushes, they sent the guards in to clear them away. Polly tried her best to persuade the Snells to let the cub settle in and gain his confidence before he was put on show, but they were too impatient.

They announced that the "grand opening" would be the next day and they were expecting hundreds and hundreds of people to buy tickets. Polly felt very nervous about it. There would be crowds of strangers, flashing their cameras, making videos, shrieking, laughing, clapping –

so much noise. It would be very frightening
for poor little Booboo.

She managed to persuade the Snells to
allow Stan to help her get everything ready. She
hoped that, between them, they might make the
enclosure feel more homely for the cub and that
would help him to deal with all the people. When
Polly took Stan to meet Booboo and explained
that he wanted to help, the cub took to him
immediately, and they became friends.

Stan cleaned out the pool and cut the grass.
He swept out the little concrete house and hung
an old tyre up in the plastic tree. Booboo ran and
jumped onto it straight away, and he swung back
and forth in it all day. Polly felt happy and sad

at the same time. She was
pleased to see him being a
bit more courageous.

In the evening,
she tucked Booboo
up in his bed
and kissed him
goodnight.

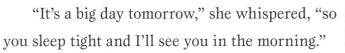

"It's a big day tomorrow," she whispered, "so
you sleep tight and I'll see you in the morning."

She didn't like leaving, but Crow would
stay with him.

Polly didn't look forward to the walk
home. It was when she was most aware of the
roaring and she hated it. It was closer and louder
than ever. As soon as she left the gates of the zoo,
she felt completely spooked, as if someone, or
something, was watching her … following her…
Though when she turned around, no one was there.

As she was getting ready for bed, Polly stared
out at the green expanse of fields beyond the high

Abbeville walls. She could see a distinct track trampled into the long grass among the hedgerows, snaking through the next field, and the next. It looked as if it came all the way from Wild Bear Woods, and Polly knew what that meant. Someone was coming from Wild Bear Woods to Abbeville and that could only be a bear – and, judging by the size of the track, that bear was not alone.

Polly couldn't get to sleep that night. Her head was full of jumbled thoughts, racing. She couldn't stop thinking about those tracks in the grass, and there were strange noises from outside too: dogs barking and loud crashes of dustbins being turned over.

It must have been in the early hours of the morning that Polly finally fell asleep, before she was woken by a nightmare. It felt so horribly real that at first she wasn't sure if she was still dreaming. The whole room was vibrating with sound. It was a kind of hoarse breathing, husky and guttural, and she knew it must be the bears. It felt like they were all around her, in the house, in the walls, padding across the floors, their great thick fur brushing up against the banisters, their claws scoring deep tracks along the wallpaper.

Polly's eyes snapped open. She was alone in her room. She pushed back the duvet and tiptoed across the carpet. She held her breath as she drew the curtain, just far enough to peer out. The street was empty, but under the streetlamp, a large black shadow moved and disappeared around the corner. Polly shivered with fear.

CHAPTER 12

Next morning, Polly was scraping the last soggy cornflakes from her bowl, when there was a newsflash on the radio.

"There are reports that four adult bears were in Abbeville late last night after a breach of the town boundary walls."

Polly almost choked on her cereal.

The newsreader went on, "Witnesses say that the bears, which were 'huge and hairy, with dreadful eyes and horrible teeth', scaled the wall at its lowest point on the eastern side of the town.

It is believed that they were headed for the bear enclosure at the zoo. The owners, Mr and Mrs Snell, have confirmed, however, that there were no intruders last night, and their baby bear remains safe ahead of today's grand opening of the Bear Garden."

Poor Booboo, thought Polly. Perhaps it would have solved everything if the bears had succeeded and taken him. She wondered if he'd heard his family from his little concrete bedroom.

The newsreader continued, "There is growing concern in the town of Abbeville about the danger of keeping a bear in the zoo. Several people have contacted this news channel."

At this point the newsreader took a call from a member of the public who wished to remain anonymous.

"Well, they're dangerous, aren't they?" she said. "I mean, even a baby one. You don't know what it might do. And what if it escaped? What about our children? It doesn't bear thinking about…" The caller tailed off and the newsreader continued.

"Police are advising the public to carry on as usual, but to be vigilant and to report anything suspicious. They have reassured this news channel that the bears have now left the town. There have been no more reports of damage to persons or property, apart from two lamp posts, close to the walls of the zoo, which have fallen over."

Polly quickly turned the radio off as her parents came into the kitchen. She was glad they hadn't heard the news report. They would have been worried and might have stopped her from going to the zoo. Neither she nor Stan had told them about the bear cub, although, with the grand opening today, it was unlikely they'd be able to keep it a secret much longer. After her parents had left for the restaurant, Polly rushed out.

She found a huge crowd of people gathering at the zoo gates.

Some were holding placards.

"NO MORE BEARS!"

"GET RID OF THE BEAR!"

They looked angry.

"Oh, dear," said Polly.

As she went on towards the Bear Garden, Polly passed the Snells' office. She didn't want to stop but couldn't help herself. It sounded as though the Snells were having a row. Through the window, Polly saw Mr Snell running round and round his desk, clutching his head.

"I told you! I told you! I told you it was bonkers!" he sobbed. "Now everyone is angry and we're going to lose all our money and we're going to be eaten by bears!"

Polly looked at Mrs Snell. Her eyes were glittering, and she was smiling. "Albert!" she shouted and clapped her hands together.

Mr Snell stopped and jerked his head round to look at her. Then he stifled a sob and began to run again.

"Albert! Albert! You fool! Get a grip!" shouted Mrs Snell. "As usual, you are wrong. Completely wrong. This is brilliant! This is the best thing that could have happened … we're on the news! It's the best publicity we could ask for! Everyone will come to see our baby bear now. A baby bear in a magnificent enclosure, locked up with guards all round him. Scary, but also perfectly safe."

"But they're so cross!" Albert shouted. "They're scared of bears and they want us to get rid of this one!"

"You just wait!" Mrs Snell gave a knowing little grin.

Polly raced to the Bear Garden, where she found Booboo and Crow. Booboo was very confused by all the noise and all the people – he could see them from the top of his climbing frame. Polly and Crow did their best to reassure him. He didn't seem to know anything about the bears' visit last night. (Polly guessed he must have been sound asleep in the concrete hut while they were rampaging around.) Just as well, she thought. She decided not to tell him about the visit. It was best that he didn't get his hopes up.

The crowd outside the zoo grew larger and angrier as the morning went on. Finally, Mrs Snell went out to greet them. She didn't say anything – she just smiled and opened the gates. People rushed inside, shouting and waving their placards, as Mrs Snell calmly led them, without their knowledge, to the Bear Garden. At first, there were cries and shouts of fear at the sight of

the bear cub in the enclosure. Booboo tried to hide
behind the plastic tree, but as the shouting began
to die down, he came out from behind the tree
and climbed into his hammock. He gazed up at the
crowd with his big brown eyes, and there was an
awed silence from the crowd.

"Oooh," someone whispered. "He's so cute!" And then everyone was whispering, because he was just a baby – a sweet, little, adorable, furry baby. They cooed, they took photographs, they called out to him, they threw him nuts and sweets. They were thrilled to see him.

"He's not like a real scary bear at all!" they said. "He's adorable! We must keep him here! We'll protect him from the other bears – those dreadful, scary creatures!"

Mrs Snell's smile grew wider and wider. "See?" she said to Mr Snell, who had crept up the steps of the platform to join his wife. "I told you!"

Polly, who was still inside the enclosure with Booboo, couldn't believe it. "Look at them smiling! They really like you," she told him.

They certainly did! They loved him! They gasped and cheered and clapped as he ran around his garden with Polly and Crow.

At closing time, Booboo watched the people go with a funny expression on his face. Polly tucked him up in bed and kissed him goodnight. "See you tomorrow, little fellow," she said.

"Will they come back?" asked the cub, as she was closing the door to his hut.

Polly stopped. Did he mean the bears? Did he know they'd tried to find him? "Who, Booboo?" she asked.

"All those people," answered Booboo. "Will they come back tomorrow?"

"Oh, yes!" said Polly. "I'm sure they will. Would you like that?"

Booboo nodded his head sleepily and tucked his nose under his arm and Polly saw again how small and lonely he was. With a heavy heart, she closed the door and tiptoed away.

If she hadn't felt so anxious, Polly would have told herself that the day had gone well, despite everything about it being so wrong. Booboo had coped brilliantly. He'd even enjoyed it. But another night was coming. Would it bring the bears again? They hadn't hurt anyone last night, though by now they must be desperate, and that would make them even more dangerous.

On her way out of the zoo, Polly passed the office again. She could see Poodywoo lying in a pool of evening sunlight on the desk. Mr Snell was standing, staring out of the open window. He turned towards Polly, beaming, as he snipped the tip off a fat cigar. Then he lit it and puffed a cloud of smoke out at her.

"A successful afternoon, I think, Polly!" he said. "High-five!"

He stretched a scrawny hand through the window. Reluctantly, Polly touched the tips of his fingers with her own and tried to smile.

"Congratulations, Mr Snell," she said.

 CHAPTER 13

For the next week, it looked as though Mr and Mrs Snell were going to be right about everything. Despite being terrified of bears, everyone wanted to see a baby one. And there hadn't been any more reports of bears in the town at night.

The ticket sales at Happy Days Zoo went through the roof! Ice-cream sales soared, postcard sales soared, everything soared, especially the moods of Mr and Mrs Snell.

Mr Snell pranced around the zoo, greeting people, being helpful, grinning, grinning, grinning and cracking corny jokes. He was everybody's best friend. Polly found it hard to watch. He might as well have carried a sign saying, "I've made it! I'm a success! I'm going to be very, very rich!"

And Mrs Snell... Well, she spent as little time at the zoo as possible. She mostly went to the hairdresser and the nail parlour, which gave her plenty of time to think and plan. Now that the zoo was really going to make a profit, some of her dreams might actually come true.

Clever Mr and Mrs Snell. People absolutely loved the bear cub. They queued around the block to see him. They came in droves – uncles, aunts, cousins, grandparents – everyone came, just as Mrs Snell had said they would! They ahhed, they cooed. Whatever the cub did, the crowd went,

"Awwww!" and recorded it to show their friends. People came for feeding time, for bathing time, for grooming time, for any old time at all. They even queued to watch Booboo sleep.

They began to bring presents – a ball, a rubber ring, a hula hoop. The cub loved the presents. He ran about, kicking the ball, throwing it, catching it. He started to show off. He rolled the ring along his arms and flicked it, so it landed on his nose. The crowd went crazy! They loved him so much.

"Why have we been so worried about bears all this time?" they said. "They're so sweet!"

The presents began to get bigger and more expensive, and Booboo's fans competed with each other as to who could bring the best. They brought a climbing frame with ropes and a slide. They brought a Wendy house. They brought a canoe, a scooter and a trampoline. They brought games, a computer and even a giant flat-screen TV.

Every day was like a birthday and each morning the cub rushed out of his hut to see what was coming next. Where would it all end?

Polly was worried. She loved to see Booboo so happy, but the feeling never lasted. Each evening, as the crowds began to leave, the little bear grew anxious again. He would watch the people collecting their children, picking up their bags, and he would start running up and down, crying.

Polly tried to make sure she was always there, with Crow, to comfort him. The cub would throw himself into her arms and wail, "I want my mummy!" and for the millionth time, Polly wished she could take him home.

One evening like this, Mrs Snell was lurking outside the concrete hut in the Bear Garden. She was spying on Polly. She often did. She liked to crouch below the window of the hut and eavesdrop. On this particular evening, she heard something that made her blood run cold. Polly was putting the cub to bed, tucking him in, kissing him goodnight, when Mrs Snell heard her say, "They will come, Booboo. I promise you."

"But how do you know?" asked the little bear.

Here, Polly had hesitated, and Mrs Snell had raised her head to peer through the glass.

"Because they aren't far away," Polly said in the end. "They're nearly here."

Mrs Snell could see that Polly's hand was trembling as she spoke.

Mrs Snell pressed herself against the damp wall and listened for more...

"You just have to wait a little longer, Booboo," said Polly. "I've heard them, I really have, and I know they're coming for you, so you must be patient."

Mrs Snell clutched her beating heart. She'd been sure they were plotting something. That girl... She'd known she was bad news! It's high time she went home – and there'll be no more time spent alone with that cub.

"MOLLY!" she bellowed, walking to the door of the concrete hut. "Out you go, Molly! Closing time!"

Polly jumped at the sound of Mrs Snell's voice, before glancing back at the cub.

He had fallen asleep. She hurriedly kissed him goodnight and departed, with Crow on her shoulder.

When she was gone, Mrs Snell left the enclosure, where she found two of the guards standing, bleary-eyed and tired, outside the gates.

"Falling asleep!" she cried. "No wonder Holly is plotting to steal my cub! You're dismissed! This instant! Get out of my zoo!"

So, the guards wandered home. Mrs Snell would just have to guard the cub herself. She clenched her fist round a baton and whacked it hard against the railings.

"Whoever dares to come this way," she said out loud, "be it bear or be it human, I'll be here to greet them, and NO ONE … NOTHING gets past me!"

As the zoo gates were locked, only the guards at the main exit remained. Mrs Snell stood in charge of the Bear Garden. Alone.

The moon rose higher and higher in the sky. Long blue shadows lay along the grass. Nothing stirred around the town. The animals in the zoo snoozed and snored and rolled over onto their backs, while Mrs Snell stood her ground and frowned into the darkness.

 CHAPTER 14

It was another night of very little sleep for Polly. The noise of the bears seemed to be louder than ever, their roaring reverberated, deep and booming, all around her. She was glad when morning came and she could get up and go to the zoo.

She ran all the way – down the street and up the hill. From below, she could see blue lights flashing and when she reached the gates there were police cars outside, parked at crazy angles. Instead of guards, police officers were standing at the entrance, and, stretched across the gate, was a police tape with the words "DO NOT CROSS" written on it.

With a rising sense of dread, Polly tried to go into the zoo, but a police officer asked her to explain who she was. She tried to find out what had happened, but the officer would only say that there had been an "incident" at the bear enclosure. Once the officer had cleared her to go inside, Polly ran to the Bear Garden.

The entrance to the enclosure was festooned with police tape as well, and many more police officers were there. Some were patrolling in pairs. Others were standing around doing very little,

while yet more, dressed in white overalls from head to toe, were combing the ground, putting tiny things into plastic bags and writing labels. Polly guessed that they were the forensic team, and, like she'd seen on TV, they were collecting important evidence. But evidence of what? What had happened?

At last, Polly spotted Stan talking to an officer. She ran over to him.

"Ah, Polly," said Stan. He turned to the officer. "This is my niece, Polly Pecorino. She looks after the bear cub."

"Good morning, miss," said the officer.

"Is Booboo all right?" she cried. "What's happened? Is Booboo safe?"

Stan put his arm around Polly. "Booboo is fine," he said. "Absolutely fine. It's Mrs Snell."

"What is?" asked Polly. "What has she done?"

"It's not what she's done, Polly. It's what's happened to her. I'm afraid it's very serious," said Stan.

"Very serious indeed," agreed the officer.

"What is it?" asked Polly. "Tell me! Please tell me, Uncle Stan!"

For a moment, she was worried that Mrs Snell had gone into the Bear Garden and Booboo had attacked her, or something like that, though she could hardly imagine such a thing.

"I don't want you to be alarmed, Polly," said Stan. "Everything's under control. We are all perfectly safe, as you can see." He gestured towards the police officers that were standing around. "But I'm sorry to have to tell you that the bears from Wild Bear Woods came here last night … and … and Mrs Snell is missing!"

"Missing!" cried Polly.

"Along with the cat," said the officer.

"Poodywoo?" asked Polly.

"Yes, Polly. I'm afraid so," said Stan. "The bears must have tried to get into the Bear Garden and they found Mrs Snell and Poodywoo outside … and then they…" He gulped. "They… Oh, Polly…"

Polly didn't need him to finish his sentence. She looked at the gate. It was covered in deep scratches, as if the bears had tried to tear it apart. Polly felt sick.

"But didn't anyone see anything?" she asked the officer, when she'd recovered from the initial shock. "Have you found any sign of them?"

"Nothing yet, miss. Our team are on it," said the police officer. "You'd better go and check on that cub."

"May I?" said Polly.

"Off you go!" said Stan. "I saw him this morning, but I know he'll want to see you too."

Before she went, Polly took a closer look at the

gate and the marks on it. It was scored all
over with great gouges made by claws, sharp
as skewers.

"Those marks
are weird, Stan.
They look almost
like a drawing,"
she said.

"Terrifying! I can
hardly look at them!" said Stan. "Now, go and
check on Booboo, will you?"

At first, Polly couldn't see the cub anywhere.
Then she saw him. He was sitting on the highest
point of the climbing frame, rocking back and
forth, and gazing out beyond the walls of the zoo.

Polly realized that he could probably see all
the way to Wild Bear Woods.

"Hello, Booboo," she said. "Are you coming
down, or shall I come up?"

The cub shifted along the bar he was sitting

on to make room for Polly. She carefully climbed
up and they sat, side by side, staring out.

"I want to go home," he sighed. "I want my
mummy... Where's my mummy? Why don't they
come and get me?"

Polly held her breath. Should she tell him that the bears had come for him twice now? Wouldn't he just be dreadfully disappointed that they'd got so close and failed? And how would she explain what they'd done to Mrs Snell and Poodywoo? Maybe best not to say anything, she thought.

"I'll get you home, Booboo," she said. "I promise. I'm going to find a way."

The cub leaned against Polly and she put her arm around him. "Don't worry," she said. "Everything's going to be fine."

She hoped she sounded more convinced than she felt.

 # CHAPTER 15

Later, Polly went to look for Mr Snell to see
if there was anything she could do to help.
She found him in his office with the detective
inspector of the police. Mr Snell was dreadfully
upset, weeping and blowing his nose into
squares of paper towel.

"How could they? How could they do this?"
he wailed. "Oh…"

Polly introduced herself to the detective and
they both watched Mr Snell rummage in the top
drawer of his desk, neither knowing what to say.

"Where is it? Oh, where is it?" he cried.

He pulled the drawer out completely and

tipped the contents onto the floor. Torn receipts, chewed pens, a mouldy tie, sweet papers and a pair of broken spectacles all went flying until, at last, he found what he was looking for and raised it to his lips. It was a tattered photograph. Mr Snell clutched it to his chest.

"Is that your wife, sir?" asked the detective. "May I have it? It would help us with our enquiries."

Mr Snell only held it tighter. "It's all I have left."

The detective sighed sympathetically.

"Mr Snell," he said, "I understand how difficult this is for you, but we are going to need a recent photograph of your wife, or at least a detailed description."

Mr Snell moaned. "Beautiful soft hair. Ash blonde, with a few stripes…" he said.

"Very good," said the detective in an encouraging voice. He wrote it down in his notebook. "Eye colour?"

"Green," said Mr Snell. "Glorious green, like emeralds, and perfect ears. Two beautiful ears…"

"Two, that's good," said the detective. "Any other distinguishing features?"

"Lovely long eyelashes." Mr Snell had a faraway look on his face. "And the longest whiskers I've ever seen."

"Whiskers?" said the detective. He looked confused, and then the realization came to him. He reached forwards to take the photograph from Mr Snell, but Mr Snell ducked away, leaning so far back in his chair that the whole thing

tipped up and he fell, his legs bicycling in the air, reminding Polly of an insect she had once rescued. The detective snatched the photograph.

The picture was not of Mrs Snell. It was a picture of the cat.

The detective slammed his notebook down on the desk.

Mr Snell jumped and sat up straight. "You've got to find him!" he cried, dissolving into tears again.

"Mr Snell!" said Polly. "You've got to try to help the police to find your wife!"

Mr Snell pulled out the photograph of Poodywoo from the detective's notebook and slipped it into his top pocket. "Yes, yes, by all means, Polly," he muttered. "You do whatever you think. Help the inspector. Thank you. Thank you so much!"

Then he stood up and held the door open for them. "Interview terminated at ten-oh-six hours!" Mr Snell snapped.

The detective raised an eyebrow at Polly as they walked out. Mr Snell closed the door behind them.

 CHAPTER 16

Perhaps if the police had issued a statement of some sort, there might have been less anxiety in Abbeville. As it was, everyone had seen the police cars racing up the hill and heard the sirens blaring. Everyone knew something had happened at the zoo, but they didn't know what, so all kinds of rumours were spreading about the bears. They spread like a swarm of bees gathering in a black cloud over the town.

Nobody went out any more. They hardly even dared go to the shops in the daytime, let alone to restaurants at night. The Pecorinos weren't affected, because their restaurant was in a different town that didn't have a zoo or any problems with bears, and they left home early in the morning and got back late most days. But for the rest of Abbeville, it was a different story. Even the last remaining security guards at the zoo had given in their notice. Mr Snell hadn't paid them anyway, and they didn't think it was worth risking their lives for nothing. The town itself was very quiet too and no one came to the zoo that day.

The darling cub had lost its appeal. Its darling precious snout, its shiny black nose, its twinkling brown eyes were no longer charming. It was a BEAR, after all. Not a teddy bear. It was a real wild cub and it would grow into a real wild bear.

Meanwhile, Crow was jittery and jumped at the slightest thing. Poor Polly felt more anxious than ever too. Booboo was so unhappy, and she knew it was only a matter of time before the bears came back. She absolutely didn't want anyone else in Abbeville to get hurt, so she made a decision. She had no other choice.

CHAPTER 17

"I'm going to take Booboo back to Wild Bear Woods!" Polly told Stan.

Stan didn't say anything at first, but eventually he nodded, a slow, sad nod. "I had a feeling you were going to say that." He put his hands on her shoulders. "I don't want you to do this. And I wish I could come with you."

"But you can't leave the animals," Polly said firmly, and Stan nodded even more sadly than before.

"You must leave the cub outside the woods. Don't even think about going in yourself. Just leave him there and they will find him.

Then come straight back. OK?"

It was easy to get the cub out of the zoo, with no guards around. Nobody stopped them. Nobody checked them. There was no one left – only Stan, who was waiting at the exit to say goodbye. He gave Polly a rucksack.

"It's just a few things," he said. "Water, crisps, chocolate, orange juice, a pair of scissors, a rope…"

"Thanks, Uncle Stan," said Polly.

The little bear was dancing up and down on his toes with excitement. "Home!" he kept saying. "Home! Home! Home!"

"Don't forget," said Stan. "Just leave him outside the woods and turn around and come straight back. Promise?"

"I promise," said Polly.

"And you'd better have this. It's hot today, and you don't want to get sunstroke." He put his hat on Polly's head and kissed her. Then he hugged the cub and said goodbye.

Polly, Crow and Booboo walked on down the hill through Abbeville, Crow flying ahead and then swooping back to land on Polly's shoulder. When they passed the police station with its blue lamp, Polly wondered if there was anyone in there, working on the Snell case. It certainly didn't look like it.

 CHAPTER 18

The sky was like a pale blue china bowl hanging over the dark lake. Dense trees reflected along the far edge of the water in a black lacy fringe. It seemed very quiet. Even Booboo and Crow had stopped chattering, and Polly hadn't heard a sound from the bears for ages. Their silence since the night before was unnerving. What were they doing? Perhaps – she shuddered at the thought – perhaps bears, like lions and tigers, slept after they'd feasted...

Polly had never been so close to Wild Bear Woods. She could see the path trimming the water and the fork where it went deep between the

trees and disappeared. They still had a way to go
– halfway round the lake – and Polly's heart was
already thumping hard in her chest. Crow didn't
like it here either. He'd grown more agitated the
further from home they'd got.

"Home! Home!" he cawed.

"Don't be silly, Crow!" said Polly.
"We're taking Booboo home."

The crow hopped from foot to
foot, shaking his head. "Not for
crows!" he cawed.

"It's not for me either!"
said Polly. "But we've got to
do it. So, are you going to
help me or not?"

With a squawk, the crow lifted his wings and
spiralled up, then down, and crashed onto Polly's
shoulder again. He rubbed his head against her
and nuzzled her ear with his great black beak.

"Silly old Crow," said Polly, but she felt braver
having him with her.

Then, out of the corner of her eye, she saw something moving on the road behind them. It looked like a scarecrow running, hopping, running again, its arms circling. "Wait! Polly! Wait!" it cried.

Polly's heart sank. It was Mr Snell.

The cub took one look at Mr Snell and galloped down the road, pulling Polly after him. Crow launched an attack on Mr Snell, diving from a height, skimming his head while Mr Snell shrieked and batted him with his fists.

"Polly! Polly! Polly! WAIT!" Mr Snell screamed.

He sprinted after her, threw himself on the ground at her feet and seized her ankles. "You can't go!" he spluttered. "You can't go without me! I am coming to get Poodywoo!"

"But, Mr Snell, we're only leaving the cub at the edge of the woods," said Polly.

"Nope!" hissed Mr Snell. "We're going to get Poodywoo!" He was gripping Polly's ankles very tightly.

"It's too dangerous," said Polly, thinking that Poodywoo was probably already dead – eaten – long gone, anyway. She gulped and pushed the thought away.

"If you won't let me come with you, I'll take the bear back to the zoo!" cried Mr Snell. He jumped up and lunged at Booboo. The little bear squealed.

"OK! OK, Mr Snell!" cried Polly. "You can come with us!"

He was the last person she needed right now, but she couldn't think what else to do.

They set off again, Mr Snell humming to

himself, in a world of his own. Polly noticed he was wearing odd shoes – one black and one brown. His trousers looked as if they might belong to somebody else – they were several inches too short and tied around his waist with string – and his hair was sticking up in spikes. Crow was fascinated by it and kept swooping low over the top of Mr Snell's head.

"Leave him alone!" hissed Polly. "I need you to be sensible today. Besides, I don't think Mr Snell is feeling quite himself and we should try to be kind to him."

With a squawk, Crow dropped down onto her shoulder again.

Booboo glanced at Mr Snell nervously from time to time, while Crow flew ahead, circling back regularly, keeping a lookout. The silence was eerie. Polly thought it was almost worse than the roaring she'd had inside her head, because even though

she couldn't see any bears, she felt sure they were
being watched, and they still had at least half a
mile to go before they reached the woods.

 CHAPTER 19

By the time they'd rounded the edge of the lake, the sun was at its highest, beating down on them. Polly was grateful to have Stan's hat.

Mr Snell wasn't wearing a hat and Polly had noticed his face was bright red. He had been walking more and more slowly, and the last time she'd looked, he'd been way behind. When she turned to check on him again, he wasn't there at all! She peered further back along the road. She spotted him lying there, sprawled half in and half out of the ditch, snoring with his mouth open.

"Mr Snell!" said Polly, walking towards him.

Mr Snell sat bolt upright. "Present and correct!" he said. Then he jumped up and straightened his clothes.

"Ready?" asked Polly.

"Feel a bit funny," he shouted, as if Polly were very far away.

"I think you might have sunstroke. Wear this hat."

Mr Snell put it on. Then he noticed Booboo, as if for the first time. "BEAR!" he screamed. "BEAR! BEAR!"

Booboo jumped back in surprise.

"Please don't hurt me!" Mr Snell gasped. "Please! I promise I'll be good… Only don't hurt me… Please!" He was trembling all over.

Polly forced herself to put an arm around him. "There, there, Mr Snell. Don't worry. It's all right. He won't hurt you. This is Booboo, remember? We're taking him home."

Mr Snell sniffed. Then his eyes filled with tears and he wrapped his arms around Polly.

"Poodywoo!" Mr Snell cried.

"It's all right, Mr Snell. Everything's going to be all right," said Polly. "We're going to find Poodywoo. It's not much further…"

"Oh! Poodywoo!" Mr Snell wailed again.

"Now, Mr Snell," said Polly in a commanding voice. "We're getting quite close to where the bears live, and when we get there, I'd like you to do exactly as I say. I'm hoping we won't meet the bears, but if we do, I'd like you to let me do the talking. I can talk to them," she explained. "They will understand me, and I can understand them."

"Don't be ridiculous!" retorted Mr Snell.

"I'm not being ridiculous," Polly said patiently. "That's what I do – I talk to animals."

Mr Snell frowned at Polly. "I don't even know who you are! Never mind what you do!"

"Is that really true?" asked Polly, trying to hide her alarm.

Mr Snell was obviously quite unwell, but there wasn't time to worry about that now. "We're going to look for Poodywoo, Mr Snell," said Polly, hoping the cat's name would work its magic again. It did.

Mr Snell's face lit up. "Poodywoo! Oh, Poodywoo! Where is he?"

"We think he's in the woods," Polly said. "And when we get there, you're going to call him, and with any luck, he'll come, and we can leave Booboo and go home. But you've absolutely got to do as I tell you or you'll put us all in danger. We might find your wife as well. It's possible she's in there too, so we should try calling her. OK?"

"No, no, no, no! Not her!" Mr Snell whispered. "Just the cat, please, Polly." He looked so unwell and worried that Polly didn't have the heart to argue with him.

Wild Bear Woods was close now. Booboo, zigzagging as he tottered along, was squeaking with excitement. Polly wondered if he would be able to find his family. The woods looked dark and dense beyond the massive brambles that formed a great wall all around the trees, and it was so cold it felt like winter.

The path had become much rougher, broken here and there by nettles and thistles. How much further should they go? There was a clump of trees ahead and thickets of thorny bushes and brambles twisted round old stumps like mounds of barbed wire. The feeling of being watched was even stronger. Were the bears waiting in the darkness?

"Let's go quietly now," whispered Polly.

She forced her feet to keep moving forwards, even though every part of her screamed to turn back.

But Booboo was excited. His eyes were bright and beady, his snout nodded up and down as he took in all the woody smells – the smells of home.

"Come on!" he squeaked, pulling Polly after him.

"No, wait, Booboo." Polly stopped. It felt as though all the warmth of the world had been extinguished. Immensely tall trees cast a cold shadow over them. We must have already come about two hundred metres, she thought, as she stared ahead at the darkness.

"We can't go any further," said Polly. The cub pulled her arm again. "No, Booboo. I'm sorry, but I promised Stan. Mr Snell, can you call Poodywoo and see if he'll come?"

Mr Snell went on, tiptoeing forwards with giant steps.

"Mr Snell!" said Polly. "Come back! We have to stop right here!"

"You can stop if you want to," said Mr Snell over his shoulder. "You can desert my Poodywoo, my poor darling Poodywoo. You can desert my wife, for all I care. You can desert that poor defenceless baby bear, if you want to. If that's the sort of person you are, Polly…"

He didn't slow down.

"Perhaps that is the sort of person you are," he said again, this time in an annoying sing-song voice.

"Let's go HOME!" cried Crow.

"Oh, Crow," said Polly.

She looked down at the cub. He was very small – only a baby. Then she looked at the great dark woods in front of them.

"HOME!" cried Crow insistently.

"Oh, Crow," said Polly again, thinking of her promise to Stan. But the wood was so dark… What if Booboo got lost? "I'm sorry. I can't leave this little cub here. We'll have to go on."

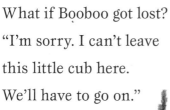

CHAPTER 20

In the deathly silence of the woods, every step they took crunched and snapped loudly. After scrambling through barricades of brambles and tangled creepers, they found themselves in an alien world where everything seemed to be dead or dying. The air felt damp – the kind of damp that seeps under your skin – and there was hardly any light. The branches overhead were woven together so tightly, it was like the domed ceiling of a cathedral. The ground was carpeted in deep swathes of dead moss and lichen and scattered with great black broken branches and spikes of ancient tree trunks.

Polly, Mr Snell and Booboo stumbled through the woods, sometimes having to feel their way. Booboo seemed happy enough, though, and Polly wondered if she should have left him, after all.

Eventually the shapes of the trees became clearer, their trunks bare. They were planted in straight rows at an equal distance apart. Now, there was a pine-needle floor beneath their feet. The branches of the trees rose higher and although they were still woven together, layer upon layer, more light filtered through.

The path was completely straight. There were no bends or twists, or even any turnings off it. It was a dead straight line, drawing them deeper and deeper into the woods. We're being swallowed up, thought Polly. It was spooky, the way everything had suddenly become so neat. The path almost looked as though it had been swept, and where a tree had fallen, there was a tidily stacked pile of logs. Then Polly noticed something that gave her a sharp jolt of fear. Hanging from a branch on one of the trees was an old picnic basket.

"Funny place to leave it!" said Mr Snell.

It wasn't funny to Polly. She shuddered as she remembered the story Stan had told her about the family who had gone picnicking in the woods. The bear's trap must have been just here.

"Booboo, do you know about the hole ... the trap?" she whispered. "Do you know where it is?"

Booboo just shrugged and skipped along in front of her. He obviously had no idea what she was talking about.

"Be careful, Mr Snell!" said Polly. "Look where you're going... There's an enormous hole somewhere and we mustn't fall into it!"

They slowed down and began to tread very carefully.

After about another ten minutes of this, Polly began to wonder if they were ever going to arrive anywhere, and after a further ten minutes, she started to think they might be in the wrong place. Could this really be where the bears lived?

"Do you remember these woods, Booboo?"
she asked. "Is this where you live? Do you
recognize it?"

The little cub chuckled and grinned at Polly.
He reached his arms over his head and jumped
up and down. "Of course! Of course!" he squeaked.

"Oh, Crow," Polly
sighed. "Will this path
ever end? Will we ever
… everrr … oooh!
Aaaarrrgh! Help!"
she cried, as the
ground beneath her
feet gave way.

She screamed! Mr Snell screamed! Booboo
shrieked!

They were falling …
down,
down,
down…
Falling
to the
depths
of the
earth.

 **CHAPTER 21**

It was dark, so dark.

"Caw! Caw!" Crow's alarm call sounded, somewhere far above them.

"Help!" shouted Polly. "Crow! Help! Do something!"

She stood up carefully – she wasn't hurt – she stretched her arms out in the darkness. The tips of her fingers found dry mossy earth. She traced it round, turning as she did so, in a circle. This must be the hole from the story. How had they not seen it?

"How stupid! How stupid of us!" cried Polly. "Now we're really in trouble."

As her eyes got used to the blackness, she saw the steep mossy walls rising up to a circle of grey light, way, way up above them.

"Crow!" she called desperately. "Crow! Where are you?"

If he replied, Polly didn't hear it, because Mr Snell had begun to moan, quietly at first, then louder and louder.

"Shh, Mr Snell, please," said Polly. "Just be quiet, so I can listen."

"I CAN'T BE QUIET!" Mr Snell yelled. "I'VE GOT TO GET OUT OF HERE!" He began to scrabble at the crumbling walls. Showers of stones and pebbles rained down on them.

"Ow! Ow! Ow!" squeaked Booboo.

Suddenly, Mr Snell cried out again. He came crashing down on top of Polly, followed by a small avalanche of rocks. A large one hit him on the side of his head. He yelped with pain. Then he went quiet.

"Mr Snell...?" said Polly. "Mr Snell! Are you all right?"

He didn't reply. He had passed out.

Polly drew the little bear to her and put her arms round him. "What shall we do, Booboo? Do you know how to get us out of here?" she whispered.

Just then, there was a squawk from above. It was Crow.

"They're coming!" he cried. "They're coming!"

Polly froze. She knew exactly who he meant.

The cub began to tremble with excitement. He threw his head back and gave a series of short, sharp cries. Polly had never heard him make those sounds before. He sounded like a real bear – not the cub she knew. She was very, very afraid.

CHAPTER 22

Polly's heart was hammering in her ears and the cub's cries were growing more piercing and shrill. There were other noises overhead now – deep voices and the thud of heavy footsteps.

Polly pressed herself against the wall and squinted upwards. She could feel warm air coming towards her. It had a fishy smell. It was bear breath! She could see the outline of the enormous head and shoulders of a bear – its great snout sniffing from side to side as it searched for them.

She gripped Booboo
in fear.

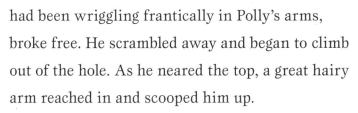

"I'm here! I'm
here!" screamed the
cub. "Help me! Help!"

The bear above them
roared, and Booboo, who
had been wriggling frantically in Polly's arms,
broke free. He scrambled away and began to climb
out of the hole. As he neared the top, a great hairy
arm reached in and scooped him up.

Polly was alone, with only Mr Snell for
company.

Meanwhile, the bears were making so much
noise – howling and roaring, while Booboo

shrieked excitedly – that Polly
couldn't make out what they
were saying. Then everything
went quiet again. Had the bears
gone? Please let them be gone,
she wished silently.

But which was worse? To be left to die and rot at the bottom of a hole, or to be dragged out and eaten? Surely Booboo would explain everything to the bears? Surely he would tell them that she had tried to help him?

Suddenly, there was another fierce growl from above. Polly trembled.

"Mr Snell! Mr Snell!" she whispered. She prodded him with her foot. "Wake up!"

The walls were shaking and raining pebbles and she couldn't see. She felt something catch at her shoulder, then her waist. Polly gasped. It was a paw. A huge bear paw, with rough pads and long sharp claws. It hooked her as easily as if she were a small silvery fish and drew her up to the surface.

She kept her eyes squeezed shut. She felt the temperature change as she rose towards daylight and then she felt the open air on her face and the dry floor of the woods on her hands.

When she finally opened her eyes and looked up, she was staring straight into two rows of perfect, gleaming white teeth.

CHAPTER 23

There were two bears glaring at Polly with their fierce, dark eyes. They looked extremely angry and one of them was growling quietly.

The larger of the two swiftly grabbed her around the waist again, lifted her off the ground and began to carry her towards the trees. Polly squirmed and kicked, but his grip was firm. She opened her mouth to speak but she was so frightened, she couldn't get the words out. The bear was almost squeezing all her breath out of her.

There was a flap of something dark close to Polly's face. It was Crow. He had swooped at the bear, his beak snapping open and shut. The bear didn't even break step. Crow swooped up again and dived down, darting at the enormous bear once more. The bear ignored him and marched on grimly, followed by the other bear who had dragged Mr Snell out of the hole and had him slung over his shoulder.

"Please!" cried Polly. "Stop! Let me explain!"

The bears ignored her. Crow kept darting down, but they seemed not to notice him.

Polly knew that, to the bears, she was the enemy. They thought she had kidnapped the cub. Why wouldn't they? They probably hated all humans. Or maybe none of that mattered and they simply wanted to eat her and Mr Snell.

Where had Booboo gone? Had his parents whisked him away? Polly knew Booboo was probably their only hope now. If only she could talk to him. But the wood was so big, he could be anywhere by now. Maybe she'd never see him again.

They were going deeper and deeper into the wood.

"It is swallowing me up," Polly said aloud. "And then I'm going to be properly swallowed up."

Stan told me not to go into the woods, she thought. I should have listened to him. Oh, Stan, I'm so sorry… Polly's heart lurched again as she thought of her parents. Poor Mum, poor Dad. They'll be so upset… Their only child, eaten by bears… Just then, she heard voices. Polly looked up and saw that they'd come to a clearing. On the other side of it, a great line of bears was standing. They were all different shapes and sizes. Each one bowed its head as they approached.

Polly tried to count them as she passed, but she was distracted by something… A hat – one of the bears was wearing a large floppy hat. Polly recognized it at once! It had belonged to Mrs Snell. Then she noticed that another smaller bear was

wearing a bracelet. It also looked familiar. Where had she seen it before?

At that moment, Mr Snell noticed it too and began to scream. "My cat's collar! It's wearing my cat's collar! They've eaten him!"

And then Polly realized. The bear was wearing on its wrist the collar that had once belonged to Poodywoo.

Polly felt as though she might faint. This was proof, if she'd needed any, that Mrs Snell and the cat had been eaten by bears. They were terrible, terrible creatures, bloodthirsty … ruthless. She hadn't wanted to believe it possible, because of Booboo, but now she did.

She had never been fond of Mrs Snell – or the cat – but what a dreadful way to die. Nobody deserved that. She was afraid she might cry, so she dug her nails into her arms as hard as she could. She'd never, ever been so frightened.

The bear that had been carrying her set her down on the ground with a bump. Polly only just managed to stay on her feet. When she looked up, Polly saw another group of bears coming through the trees. At the front of the procession was a bear beating on a drum, a slow rhythmic beat. The sight of it was so unexpected that it sent a chill through Polly.

Behind the drummer marched the largest bear of all. He was gigantic. He moved majestically through the crowd and sat down on what looked like some kind of throne. Then he gave a loud bellowing roar and Polly's legs almost gave way in terror.

# CHAPTER 24

Silence fell over the assembly. Polly stood between two bears, feeling very small. They faced the throne, which was massive. It looked very strong – it would have to be strong to take the weight of the enormous creature that sat on it, Polly thought. Perhaps this was the king of the bears.

Some bears stood in a line by the throne. There were two who seemed to be holding a tray between them, while another held a large stick. This bear stepped forwards. He thumped the ground three times with it and shouted, "Raise your paws and voices for our emperor!"

There was a deafening roar from the whole party of bears. The bear with the stick waved it like a conductor's baton, signalling to them to stop, and silence fell again. The only sound came from Mr Snell, who was somewhere behind Polly, moaning monotonously.

The emperor stood. "Have you got anything to say for yourself?" he asked Polly.

All the bears turned their eyes towards her.

Polly opened her mouth, but before she could utter a word, Mr Snell fell on his knees in front of the emperor, his forehead touching the ground.

"Your Majesty! Your Royal Highness! Your Worshipful!" he gasped. "I'll do anything … anything you want… Anything at all… Only, please, please, don't eat me…"

Polly knew that none of the bears could understand a word he was saying. They were leaning forwards, watching him. Some were growling. Some were smacking their jaws together, grinding their teeth.

Mr Snell tried again. "Your Majesty!" he began. "I'm a humble accountant. Not interesting, not tasty at all… Look at me – I'm just skin and bones…"

"Who is this person?" the emperor broke in impatiently.

Polly was afraid that Mr Snell was going to make everything even worse. He was obviously irritating the gigantic bear. She had to do something – at least the bears would be able to understand her. She raised her hand and took a deep breath.

"Excuse me," she said. "You asked me if I had anything to say…" Her voice came out in little squeaks.

"Speak up!" roared the emperor.

Polly took another deep breath and tried to steady herself. The bears were moving restlessly around her, grumbling and growling. Mr Snell had begun to moan again, and the emperor was digging his long yellow claws into the arm of his throne.

She tried once more. "I think there's been a misunderstanding," she said.

The bear with the stick suddenly leaped to attention and thumped the ground again. "Proper procedure!" he growled. "First things first! State your name!"

"Quite right!" agreed the emperor, leaning back on his throne.

"P–P–P–Polly," Polly stammered.

"P–P–P–Polly?" echoed the bears.

"That's an unusual name!" said the emperor. "P–P–P–Polly!"

"No, it's Polly," Polly said, as steadily as she could manage. "Um … how do you do?" she added bravely.

"I'm very well, thank you, but that is beside the point!" replied the emperor.

The whole assembly were still "P–P–P–Polly"-ing in squeaks and roars.

"SILENCE!" roared the bear with the stick. It took a while for them to settle down.

When they had, the emperor stood up again.

"P–P–P–Polly!" he roared. "The time has come to address this terrible case. The crimes you have committed are extremely serious. We accuse you of the kidnapping and imprisonment of our cub!"

"But, sir," Polly interrupted. "I am innocent! It wasn't me! I brought Booboo home... Please! You must believe me!"

The bears were mumbling to each other, shaking their heads.

"I would never, ever have done such a thing," said Polly. "I love Booboo. If you could only ask Booboo, I'm sure he would…"

"Enough," the emperor said. "It is up to the court to decide whether you are guilty or not guilty. We will put it to the vote."

"Vote! Vote! Vote!" the bears roared.

"All those who think P–P–P–Polly is guilty, raise your—" the emperor began, but before he'd finished speaking Polly heard a commotion behind her.

Booboo squeezed himself between the legs of several bears and came running towards her. He threw himself against her and hugged her.

CHAPTER 25

Behind Booboo came two more bears. They, too, rushed towards Polly and wrapped her in their arms. "How can we ever thank you?" they cried, and Polly realized that this must be Booboo's mother and father.

Booboo's father let go of Polly and bowed to the emperor. Then he addressed the whole assembly. "This is the bravest girl in the world," he said. "She has done a wonderful thing! She has saved our cub!"

This time all the bears roared and cheered.

"Silence!" roared the bear with the stick.

"Is this true?" asked the emperor, looking at Polly a little less fiercely.

"Well, I don't know about being brave," said Polly.

"She's the bravest girl in the world!" squeaked Booboo.

"So, you're not a kidnapper?" asked the emperor.

"No," said Polly.

"And you didn't imprison our cub?"

"No, sir," said Polly. "I didn't imprison the cub."

Whispers rippled around the assembly. The emperor sighed deeply and turned his attention to Booboo. "Booboo," he said. "I know you're very young, and I'm sorry to ask, but I'd like you to tell me if P–P–P–Polly is telling the truth."

The little bear let go of Polly's knees and turned to face the emperor. "Yes, sir," he said.

"The whole truth and nothing but the truth?" said the emperor.

"Yes, sir," said the cub solemnly.

"Well, who was it, then?" asked the emperor, leaning forwards to look into Polly's eyes. "Who captured our cub?"

Polly tried to think quickly. She didn't want to put Mr Snell in danger. Perhaps she could blame Mrs Snell. It was really her idea, after all – and if she had already been eaten, then it wouldn't make any difference if Polly told on her. But supposing she hadn't? What would happen to her then? The Snells hadn't actually been the ones to kidnap the cub...

Polly hesitated, before finally saying, "I don't know who kidnapped Booboo."

"And who imprisoned him?" asked the emperor.

Polly didn't answer for a long time. She didn't want to be responsible for anyone being eaten – but she couldn't lie.

"It might have been … er … well … possibly … er…" she began. But before Polly could finish her sentence, Booboo had crept up to the emperor and gestured that he wanted to say something. The huge bear leaned forwards, so that Booboo could whisper in his ear.

"Mrs Snell? You're sure about that?" the emperor asked Booboo.

Booboo nodded.

The whole assembly gasped. Polly wondered why Booboo hadn't mentioned Mr Snell's part in it, but perhaps he'd realized, like she had, that

Mr Snell would never even have thought of such a plan without Mrs Snell. And perhaps Booboo felt sorry for Mr Snell. Anyone would – he looked so confused and scared and was clearly suffering from sunstroke.

Booboo whispered something else and the emperor looked at Polly.

"And this girl was kind to you and brought you home?" the emperor said.

Booboo nodded his head excitedly.

"Well," said the emperor. "We owe you a big apology, P–P–P–Polly. Please forgive us!"

Polly let out a long sigh of relief. She still found it hard to speak, but she finally managed to say, "Thank you, sir. Of course, I will."

CHAPTER 26

The emperor heaved himself up off his throne.
His whole demeanour seemed to have changed.
He looked relaxed – in fact, the whole atmosphere
felt less tense. The emperor beckoned to the two
bears that were holding the tray and they came
over. Then he poured juice from a wooden jug
into a wooden tumbler and gave it to Polly.

"You must be thirsty," he said.

Polly took it gratefully. "Thank you, sir," she
said. The drink tasted like flowers and honey,
with a slightly woody flavour.

"It's delicious, sir!"

"Please call me Ralph,"
said the emperor.

"Only if you
call me Polly!"
said Polly.

"Polly," said Ralph.
"And who's this?"

Crow had landed on her shoulder.

"This is my brave friend, Crow," replied Polly.

Crow nuzzled her ear. They both knew he hadn't been all that brave at the beginning.

"And over there?" Ralph pointed to the cowering figure that was lying with his arms wrapped around a tree trunk. Two bears stood on either side of him.

"That's Mr Snell," said Polly. "Mrs Snell's husband."

"I wondered," said Ralph.

"He's very scared of bears," said Polly.

"Let's keep it that way!" said Ralph. Then he winked at Polly.

Polly blinked in surprise. Was that really a wink? Have I really been winked at by a bear?

"Now, I'll introduce you to some of my friends," Ralph continued.

"I don't expect you'll remember their names!"
He led her to a group of bears who had formed
a small semicircle. "This is Taylor."

Taylor bowed deeply.

"This is Pushkin."

Pushkin waved.

"This is Greta."

Greta curtseyed.

"And her sister, Wilhelmina," said Ralph.
"And this is Gregorin."

Gregorin stepped forwards and kissed
Polly's hand.

"And Hodge," said Ralph.

Hodge bent double in a bow and then hid behind Ralph. He was the smallest of the bears.

"And, finally, Booboo's parents, Mabel and Mort."

They both hugged Polly again.

Polly began to feel much less frightened. Surely nobody ate someone they'd been formally introduced to.

Crow nudged her with his beak.

"This is Crow," she said to the bears. "Say hello, Crow!"

"Hello, Crow! Hello, Crow! Hello, Crow!" said the bears.

"Oh!" said Polly. "I meant Crow should say hello to you!"

"Caw! Caw!" said the crow.

"Caw! Caw! Caw!" answered the bears and they fell about laughing.

"Caw! Caw! Caw! Caw!" cried Crow.

"Caw! Caw! Caw! Caw! Caw!" roared the bears.

It went on like that for a long time until everyone had lost count and Polly said, "Perhaps that's enough for now, Crow."

"Come," said Ralph. "Come on, Booboo! Let's go and celebrate your return!" He gently took Polly's arm. "Let me escort you. We're having a feast!"

"Feast?" asked Polly, suddenly feeling nervous again.

"Yes, we're having a special feast and you must join us," said Ralph.

"To celebrate!" said Greta.

"And because we are so, so sorry!" said Hodge.

"So, so, so sorry," said the other bears.

Polly took a deep breath and spoke very quickly before she could change her mind. "That's very kind of you," she said. "But before I go with you, I need to tell you that as well as bringing back Booboo – and I do understand if it's too late... I mean ... um... If it's not possible, of course... But ... um... We also came to collect the cat and Mrs Snell."

All the bears stopped in their tracks.

"Oh, dear," said Ralph.

Polly sensed that the atmosphere had changed again. In a small voice, she said, "Would that be possible at all?"

Ralph was no longer smiling. None of them were.

"I'm afraid, Polly, we may have a problem there," he said.

CHAPTER 27

"Have you eaten Mrs Snell and Poodywoo?" Polly blurted out.

The bears stared at Polly. They looked astonished. Hodge began to giggle, and then the others burst out laughing too.

Polly waited. She couldn't see what was so funny. How could they laugh about something so … dreadful?

"Oh, Polly!" said Ralph. "Is that what you've been thinking?"

"Well, yes," said Polly. "I've been very worried. I'm still worried… Have you? Eaten them, I mean."

"Don't be ridiculous, Polly! We don't eat people! Not unless we're very, very hungry!" Ralph laughed.

"Very, very, very hungry!" echoed the other bears.

"Really?" said Polly.

"Really!" replied Ralph.

"Really! Really! Really!" cried the other bears.

"But what about all those stories?" said Polly. "The people who never came back... The family who went for a picnic?"

"We rescued them!" said Ralph. "They fell into the old well and we pulled them out! It happens sometimes. We should cover it up, really."

"Did you?" asked Polly. "Did you actually rescue them?"

"Of course!" Ralph's eyes widened with surprise at such a question. "What else would we have done? We couldn't leave them there."

"But what happened after that?" asked Polly.

"Well, they stayed for a little while," Ralph replied. "We loved them, but they had to get back home eventually."

"Oh!" cried Polly. "That's wonderful! Oh, thank goodness!"

"Thank goodness! Thank goodness! Thank goodness!" echoed the bears.

Polly suddenly didn't know whether to laugh or cry, but at last, she could relax. She still had a few more questions, though.

"Why didn't that family tell anyone about you? They could have told everyone that you were kind, not scary. Why did they let everyone go on thinking that you eat people?"

Ralph scratched his head. "I don't know, Polly. Maybe they tried. Maybe no one would listen. It's hard to make people change their minds, and the people of Abbeville have been frightened of bears for a very long time."

"What a pity." Polly nodded quietly. Then she said brightly, "So, where are Mrs Snell and the cat?"

Ralph smiled. "Don't worry! You'll see them soon enough. They seem very happy here…" He paused and added under his breath, "For the moment."

"Are you very angry with her for taking Booboo?" Polly asked, feeling frightened all over again. Mrs Snell had done a terrible thing, but Polly didn't want her to be hurt.

"Well, Polly," Ralph began. "It's such a pity to have discovered the truth about

Mrs Snell." He sighed a deep sigh. "It was meant to be a simple swap: Booboo for Mrs Snell and the cat. Though now…"

"A swap?" Polly asked.

"Yes. When we couldn't get into Booboo's enclosure, we left you a message on the door."

"Oh!" said Polly, remembering the scratches and teeth marks. "That was a message? I didn't realize… It was a bit difficult to read…"

"You mean it was illegible, I suppose." Ralph sighed again. "It was my best writing."

"Well…" Polly smiled. "I think I understand it now."

Ralph smiled back and then immediately grew serious again. "I don't know what to do about Mrs Snell. She's so … interesting to us bears, you see. But … it's quite a shock."

Polly couldn't imagine anyone finding Mrs Snell

interesting, but she could see that Ralph was upset, so she didn't ask any more questions.

Ralph took Polly's hand. "I'll think about Mrs Snell later," he said. "Come on! Let's go and have a lovely party!"

As they walked on, the air grew warmer. Polly guessed they must be right in the middle of the woods. It had opened out and become lighter. Different kinds of trees grew here – broadleaved with brilliant green foliage. There were flowering shrubs too, and, in places, wild flowers grew like a carpet. Between the branches of blossom were patches of clear blue sky.

The bears led Polly over a neatly crafted wooden bridge and they followed a stream that flowed into a beautiful green pool. On the other side of the water were wooden huts and a large vegetable garden, where lettuce and spinach grew in perfect rows. Birdsong trilled in the treetops

and tiny blue butterflies fluttered in a cloud over the heads of the little procession. Booboo trotted along with Crow, as Mr Snell followed at a safe distance, keeping low to the ground. Polly could see that he was trying not to be noticed, while all the time looking anxiously for signs of his beloved Poodywoo. The bears gave him strange looks now and then, but mostly they just ignored him.

At the end of a path edged with lavender and rosemary, there was another clearing with two long tables in it. Both were spread with wooden plates piled high with food and bowls overflowing with fantastic fruits. There were jugs of juice, and each place was decorated with posies of wild violets. Hanging from a branch was an amazing chandelier that seemed to change shape as Polly watched, and she realized that it was a magnificent cluster of butterflies, in every colour imaginable – hundreds of them, maybe thousands. They darted and hovered in and out of a bunch of lilac blossoms hanging there. Polly thought it was the most beautiful thing she had ever seen.

She gazed at everything – the tables ready for the feast, the beautiful butterfly chandelier, the friendly faces of the bears, and the deep blue sky above.

"What a wonderful place," she said.

CHAPTER 28

Many more bears began to arrive and sit at the tables. Soon all the benches were full. Everyone stood as Ralph led Booboo and his parents to the head of one table.

"This celebration is all for you!" Ralph said to Booboo. "We have missed you so, so much!"

"So, so much!" echoed all the bears, clapping their paws and stamping their feet. When they'd stopped, Ralph raised his arms and said, "Let the feast begin!"

Polly sat between Pushkin and another bear called Watson. They both congratulated her on the rescue of Booboo and several bears raised their glasses and blew kisses. Polly smiled happily and looked around for Mr Snell. It took her a while to spot him, as he was slumped under a nearby tree. He was clearly still suffering from sunstroke and seemed to be asleep. Perhaps a nap would do him good, she thought.

Suddenly, everyone stopped talking.

Strolling down the centre of one of the tables – the one that Polly was sitting at – without a care in the world for anyone or anything, tail high, eyes glittering, was Poodywoo. As he passed, each bear stood, bowed briefly and sat down again. The cat glanced at Polly as he walked by, and his tail twitched. His pupils turned into tiny black slits.

"Poodywoo!" hissed Polly. "OFF! Get off the table!" She moved to pick him up, but as she did, Watson grabbed her arm.

"You mustn't touch him!" he whispered. "He doesn't like to be touched without permission!"

Poodywoo gave a self-satisfied twitch of his

tail, then he swiped her arm with his claws and sauntered on down the table.

"Ow!" cried Polly.

Watson smiled. "He has such sweet little claws," he said. "So small." He held out his paw and showed Polly his own enormous claws.

"Gosh!" said Polly.

"They're big, aren't they?" said Watson, pleased with Polly's reaction.

"They certainly are!" said Polly.

Meanwhile, Poodywoo had arrived at a large platter of salmon that had been perfectly cooked and exquisitely decorated with cucumber, celery and some frilly green leaves. Here, he settled on his haunches and began to eat. Polly was outraged!

"You can't let him do that!" she whispered to Watson. "That's disgusting!"

Watson just grinned at Poodywoo indulgently.

Then there was a shout from behind and Polly looked round and saw that Mr Snell had woken up. His eyes were fixed on the cat. "Poodywoo!"

he shrieked. "Poodywoo! Poodywoo!" His voice broke into sobs and tears ran down his cheeks.

All the bears stared at him in amazement, but Poodywoo didn't react at all. He had stopped eating and was sitting on the table with one leg up behind his ear, licking his bottom.

Mr Snell rushed forwards. "Oh! My darling! My angel! My only friend!" he cried.

He was in such a hurry to reach his beloved that he didn't notice a stool in the middle of the clearing. He crashed into it and landed in a heap at Polly's feet. Polly kneeled down to help him, but he seemed unfazed. He was gazing adoringly at his cat.

The cat, meanwhile, with a vague look in Mr Snell's direction, hopped off the table and slowly padded towards him.

Mr Snell stretched out his arms. "Come to Daddy!" he whispered. "Come, Poodywoo! Come to Daddy!"

Poodywoo had very little affection for Mr Snell, or anyone, but he nuzzled Mr Snell's earlobe for half a second and then sauntered away. It was enough for Mr Snell. He lay in the long grass, smiling happily.

The bears went back to celebrating. They ate to the sweet sound of birdsong rising and falling like penny whistles. Polly helped herself to some delicious blue and red berries and was just thinking how perfect it all was, and how harmonious, when suddenly everyone stopped talking again.

All eyes had turned to stare towards the far end of the table. Polly turned too. And there was Mrs Snell.

CHAPTER 29

Mrs Snell looked completely different. Instead
of the prim little French knot she usually wore,
her hair cascaded down her back. She wore a
crown of twigs, laced through with leaves and
petals and, reaching up
above the twigs, a few
poppy heads and
pheasant tail feathers
stuck out. She was
wearing an orange
bra and a grass
skirt, and a garland
of wild flowers hung
around her neck. Polly
glanced behind her at Mr
Snell. He was still lying in
the long grass but now on
his stomach, propped up
on his elbows. He looked

mesmerized. His pale bony face was creased with smiles.

Polly had to admit that Mrs Snell looked … well … almost beautiful, in a way.

The bears had obviously looked after her. Now, though, they were staring at her, having heard what she had done, and Polly could sense their hostility. How would they treat her, now that they knew she'd kept Booboo a prisoner?

Booboo shrieked and dived under the table when he saw her.

"Booboo, wait!" called Ralph. He caught the distressed cub and held him close and whispered in his ear for a long time. Finally, the cub returned to his mother and father, while still keeping a watchful eye on Mrs Snell.

Mrs Snell seemed completely unaware of it all and started to tuck into the feast. She had really disgusting manners, cramming food into her mouth with both hands. Much of it fell onto her plate and even down her top. Polly hoped the bears didn't think all humans behaved like that. But the bears seemed to find her fascinating. Even Booboo calmed down.

"She is really interesting," he said, mouth open in amazement.

Mrs Snell had not noticed Polly yet, but when she eventually pushed her plate aside and wiped her mouth with the back of her hand, she looked down the table and their eyes met.

Mrs Snell's mouth hardened into a thin red line. "What are you doing here, you little snitch?" she mouthed. "Go away!"

Polly was relieved to see Ralph coming towards her.

"What's going to happen to her?" she asked him quietly. "For what she did to Booboo?"

Ralph didn't answer for a moment. "It's time we had a talk," he said finally. "Will you walk with me?"

He took her arm and they wandered through a silvery grove of willow trees beside the stream.

"First, I want to tell you again how grateful we are," said Ralph, "for bringing Booboo safely back to us. If there's ever anything we can do to repay you… If there's anything you ever want – it's yours."

"Please, Ralph, you don't have to do anything. I'm just so happy that Booboo is home again," said Polly.

"Well, I mean it," said Ralph. "Anything. But I must talk to you about Mrs Snell."

They stopped and sat on a bench by the stream.

"I've given it some thought," said Ralph, "and I think the best thing would be if she stayed."

"Stayed?" exclaimed Polly. It was the last thing she'd expected him to say. "You want her?"

"We do, Polly. For many reasons. Let me explain." He paused and stared into the sparkling water. "We can't let her go back to town, not now that we know what she did to poor Booboo. Imagine if she tried to do something like that again! We must keep her here, so she can never hurt any other animals or their babies."

Polly couldn't help smiling at that. It was such a relief! Mrs Snell staying here with the bears would mean the animals in the zoo would be safe as well.

"And … Mr Snell?" she said hopefully. "Perhaps he should stay too?"

"I suppose he was just as bad really, was he?" asked Ralph.

"Well … not quite as bad," said Polly truthfully. "And most of the time, he was just doing what Mrs Snell told him. But he isn't at all nice to the animals in the zoo."

"Well, we'll keep him too, then," said Ralph.

"And … the cat?" asked Polly hesitantly. "Would you consider keeping the cat…? Because I happen to know he doesn't want to go home."

Ralph beamed. "We'd love to keep the cat!" he said. "We all adore the cat!"

Polly was beginning to feel almost light-headed. "But what will you do with the Snells?" she asked.

"Ah-ha!" smiled Ralph. "Well, I've thought up a very good plan! Come! Come and see my inspiration!"

He led Polly along the path until they came to an emerald-green pool. A small group of younger bears were sitting at the water's edge, their eyes round with amazement. They were watching someone dive into the water. It was Mrs Snell.

CHAPTER 30

Polly couldn't believe what she was seeing. Even after all that lunch, Mrs Snell swam like a seal, water sliding off her skin like drops of mercury. When she emerged from the water, she stood on tiptoe on the edge of the pool, her scarlet toenails like tiny exotic berries, and raised her arms. As she rose into a perfect arc and dived again, sunlight caught the spray and the drops became clusters of sparkling diamonds.

"She's like a mermaid ... so graceful," said Polly with surprise.

"Isn't she marvellous?" said Ralph.

"Well, yes!" agreed Polly. "I had no idea!"

"Really?" asked Ralph. "We thought she must be famous."

"Hmmm," said Polly. As far as she knew, Mrs Snell was only famous for her rudeness and bad temper, but she just said, "She certainly should be!"

"She will be, Polly!" said Ralph. "She definitely will be!"

"How do you mean?" asked Polly.

"This is my marvellous plan!" Ralph beamed. "We are going to keep Mrs Snell as an exhibit – just the way she kept Booboo! Bears will come from all over the country to see her perform!"

"Gosh!" said Polly. "But I think she likes swimming and diving." It didn't seem quite fair that Mrs Snell should be allowed to do something that made her happy when she'd made Booboo so miserable.

"Oh, don't worry!" Ralph smiled. "It's not all going to be splashing about. She'll have to work

too. Everyone here does – and we'll give her all the beastliest jobs. If she shows that she can be a kinder person, we'll move her onto nicer jobs. And we'll put Mr Snell to work too. Is he good at anything?"

"I don't think so," said Polly.

"Well, we'll find things for him to do. Like building the enclosure. They'll be so cosy in there together. They'll love that, won't they?" He gave a little wink.

Polly began to laugh. "That's the best punishment you could ever think of!" she said.

"Good!" said Ralph. "I must go and sort it all out now. I've chosen the perfect spot for it and I've got my team working there already. We'll get the Snells in by the end of the week and they can start work tomorrow. Once they've got into their routine, we'll have a grand opening!"

 CHAPTER 31

So, it was time to say goodbye to the Snells at last. How unusual, thought Polly, to look forward to saying goodbye. She wouldn't feel remotely sad about leaving Poodywoo either, she thought, as she watched him stroll along the path away from the clearing.

Polly saw that after finishing her swim, Mrs Snell had gone straight back to the feast and was tucking into a large plate of fruit. Mr Snell, with a bunch of grapes in one hand, was sitting beside her. He picked a grape from the bunch and held it up.

"Open wide!" he said, grinning from ear to ear.

Obediently, Mrs Snell opened her mouth and caught the grape as he tossed it. Mr Snell beamed. He threw another, and another, each one landing perfectly between Mrs Snell's open lips.

Another talent I didn't know about, thought Polly, and one that they can share! It seemed to be delighting Mr Snell. He was gazing at her in almost the same way as he gazed at his beloved cat, sometimes cooing little words of encouragement, "Clever girl! Oh! Such a clever little thing!" as each grape dropped into her mouth and slid down her throat.

How Mrs Snell felt, however, was hard to tell. She barely acknowledged Polly when she went over and told them she was leaving, but Mr Snell threw his arms around her.

"Is it really true – I can stay with Poodywoo?" he cried. "And Dolores?" he added.

Polly nodded and said that, yes, it was absolutely true.

"I never thought I could be so happy!" said Mr Snell. "I couldn't really live without him, you know, and I didn't really want to go back to the zoo at all... Oh, Polly! This is wonderful! I'm going to be a better person from now on! I'm going to try! I promise! It was the stress of that place ... it made me do things... Oh, Polly! Thank you!"

"What about the zoo, Mr Snell?" asked Polly. "What's going to happen to it?"

"I want to give it to Stan," said Mr Snell.

"Really?" asked Polly. "Are you sure?"

"We're sure, aren't we, Dol?" he said.

Mrs Snell grimaced at this affectionate shortening of her name.

"That place…" she almost spat. "That place is the most awful, filthy, money-guzzling dump I've ever been in! You tell Stan he can keep it!" she snapped. "And good luck to him! He'll need it."

"You tell Stan, Polly," said Mr Snell quietly. "He's a good man and I know he'll make a success of it."

"I will," said Polly. She looked at Mr Snell and his chaotic hair, his terrible clothes, his bony legs that seemed always to be about to buckle, and felt a wave of sympathy. He was just hopeless – not wicked. He couldn't be wicked if he could see the goodness in Stan.

"I'll tell him. Thank you, Mr Snell! Thank you, Mrs Snell! He'll be so happy!"

Polly called for Crow then. He landed on her shoulder, and together they went to say goodbye to the bears. Booboo hugged Polly and kissed Crow.

"We'll never forget you," said Booboo's mother. "Come back and see us!"

"I will," said Polly. "I definitely will."

And she knew she would.

"Please come back soon," said Ralph. He gave her a hug too. "Come back whenever you like. We'd love to see you."

With Crow on her shoulder, Polly set off for home. Watson and Hodge accompanied them as far as the edge of the Wild Bear Woods, chatting

all the way. They agreed to say farewell, instead of goodbye, because that meant they would see each other again soon.

"So, you'll come to the grand opening?" asked Watson.

"Wouldn't miss it for the world!" said Polly.

Then it was Crow's turn to say goodbye.

"Caw! Caw! Caw!" he cried.

"Caw! Caw! Caw! Caw!" cried Watson and Hodge.

The two bears stood at the edge of the woods and waved to Polly and Crow until they were far out of sight.

CHAPTER 32

When they turned up the hill to town, Polly saw someone coming towards them.

"Stan!" she cried and ran into his arms.

"Stan! Stan!" cawed Crow.

"Thank goodness!" said Stan. "Thank heavens you're safe!"

"I'm fine!" cried Polly. "Everything's fine!"

Stan held her at arm's length and looked at her carefully.

"You see?" said Polly.

"I can see you're all in one piece," said Stan, grinning. Polly laughed and took his arm. "I've got so much to tell you!"

Polly told Stan everything that had happened on her adventure. "What a wonderful ending," said Stan when Polly had finished. "I can hardly believe it! No more Snells!"

"But that's not the end of the story," said Polly.

"It isn't?" asked Stan.

"Nope!" replied Polly. Now she was finding it hard to speak because she was smiling so much.

Stan looked at her. "What?" he asked. "What is it?"

Polly made an effort to straighten her face. "Mr Snell..." Polly paused, grinning again. "Mr Snell says he wants to give the zoo to you!" she said all in a rush.

"Me?" whispered Stan.

"Yup!" said Polly.

She grabbed Stan's hands and danced him

round and round. They danced up and down the road.

Then Stan stopped. "Polly, are you sure you haven't dreamt the whole thing?"

Polly looked directly into Stan's eyes. They were so close; their noses were almost touching.

"It wasn't a dream, Stan," she said. "It's all true. The Snells have gone to live with the bears! The bears are our friends and the zoo belongs to you!"

Stan sat down on the side of the road. He took out his handkerchief and blew his nose. Polly sat beside him. They stayed there for a long while before they set off again.

 CHAPTER 33

By the time they'd reached Abbeville it was dark, and Stan and Polly had made hundreds of plans.

"We can grow our own vegetables for some of the animals," said Polly.

"And we'll give Booboo's climbing frame to the monkeys," said Stan.

"And we'll get real fish again for the penguins!" said Polly.

They had so many ideas for the zoo, but they were even more excited about telling everyone the truth about the bears.

As the news spread, people weren't sure whether to believe it or not, so Stan called a meeting in the town hall, and Polly stood onstage and told the whole story all over again.

Everyone listened in awe, and when she'd finished speaking, there was rapturous applause. The cheering was so loud you might have been able to hear it in Wild Bear Woods.

People had spent so long living in fear and worry – and it was over! It was time for fun and celebrations, music and dancing. There were only good things to look forward to – new freedom, new horizons... Perhaps even new friends!

The first thing the people decided to do was to pull down the high walls that surrounded Abbeville.

At the same time, renovations began at the zoo. Everyone was glad the Snells had gone. They had turned it into a shameful place. Every family in Abbeville agreed to become part of a new scheme, thought up by Stan, to sponsor different animals. Polly's parents chose the wild boar, or cinghiale, as it's known in Italy, because that was where Mr Pecorino came from. Their neighbours, who loved everything Australian, chose the kangaroos, and the neighbours on the other side,  gazelles. Each family chose a species that meant something to them, for whatever reason, (even the snakes found someone to care about them) and they helped to pay for good food, good bedding and any repairs that needed doing to their shelters.

Soon enough, Happy Days Zoo became worthy of its name, and every single animal was glad to live there.

CHAPTER 34

Polly and Stan and Crow were busier than ever, but after a few weeks, they took some time off to visit Wild Bear Woods for the grand opening of the Snells' enclosure. They were given a joyous welcome by the bears. Booboo and Crow were especially pleased to see each other. Polly introduced Stan to each bear, one by one, and they greeted him as if he was an old and trusted friend.

The Snells' enclosure sat in a large clearing. It had high walls, skilfully built from long narrow

tree trunks, and a raised platform that ran all the way round its base. A scratchy sign was nailed to a post. Polly guessed it was Ralph's "best handwriting" again.

"It says 'Human Beings: The Snells', before you ask." Ralph smiled.

"I knew that." Polly grinned.

There was a long queue of bears outside the enclosure – hundreds of them – they'd come from miles around. Ralph stood at the front of the steps, leading up to the viewing platform, where a ribbon had been stretched between two trees. He raised his arms and a hush fell over the crowd.

"Welcome! Welcome, everybody!" he
roared. "Thank you for coming. You won't be
disappointed! We are proud and delighted to
declare the Snells' enclosure officially open!"

He deftly cut the ribbon with a sharp claw,
and Polly and Stan and all the bears climbed
up onto the platform and looked down. Polly
gasped. Below her was an exquisite garden with
beautiful trees and flowers and a sparkling lake
in the middle. It was so much nicer than Booboo's
enclosure at the zoo had been! The bears had been
incredibly kind to the Snells.

Then the Snells emerged from the trees and stood by the lake. They began to "perform" – Mrs Snell dived and pirouetted on the shore, while Mr Snell applied himself to a series of complicated exercises, beginning with running on the spot and ending in a spectacular belly flop into the lake. This made the bears howl with laughter. Poodywoo, fast asleep under a large fern, woke with a shriek and leaped skywards with all his fur standing on end. The bears were delighted.

"It's going to be a huge success, Polly, thanks to you," said Ralph. "Now that they're used to the idea, the Snells have been doing everything they are told. And they've worked so hard on their swimming routine. I think they want to make us happy. I think you'll find they've changed!"

When she saw the Snells later, Polly had to admit, they did seem different. They were nicer. Even Mrs Snell. She actually apologized to Polly, and to Stan, for having been so horrible in the past. Not only that but she thanked them

– especially Polly. She told Polly that she was learning how to be content for the first time in her life. "The bears are so … kind." Mrs Snell sniffed. "And they really love me, you know. I … want to make them happy."

"I'm very glad, Mrs Snell," said Polly.

"Please, Molly, call me Dolores!" said Mrs Snell.

But Polly couldn't quite manage that.

Before Polly and Stan left that evening, they made plans with the bears for more visits.

"I'd like to bring my parents," said Polly.

"I'd like to bring my whole street!" said Stan. "In fact, I expect most of Abbeville would like to come!" he said.

"We'd be delighted!" Ralph said. "The more the merrier."

"The more the merrier!" echoed Hodge and Watson.

"Would you ever consider coming to visit us?" asked Polly.

"Could we?" asked Greta.

"Yes!" said Polly. "It would be wonderful!"

"Then we shall!" said Ralph.

And from that day to this, the bears of Wild Bear Woods and the people of Abbeville have been good friends and neighbours. Abbeville was one of the happiest places for miles around. People sometimes talked about "the bad old days", before the rescue of the cub, but now no child would ever have to grow up in fear of bears again. The bears were their friends.

So, if you ever see a little girl bending down to dip her fingers into a puddle of water to save a drowning fly, keep an eye on her. She's a rescuer. She may begin with saving bugs and butterflies, and even crows, but one day ... you never know ... she might just rescue a whole town.

ACKNOWLEDGEMENTS

My thanks to Laura Cecil for all her support, wisdom and friendship, and the wonderful team at Walker Books, Denise Johnstone-Burt, Annalie Grainger, Louise Jackson, Jamie Hammond, Louisa Dinwiddie and Megan Middleton.